Broken For You

Deborah Suddard

Published by Devlyn Books, 2018.

BROKEN FOR YOU

First edition. March 28, 2018.

Written by Deborah Suddard.

Dedication....

THIS NOVEL STARTED as a dream not long after the death of my friend and mentor, Dr. Mary Schaefer. She spent her life advocating for women in ministry, and encouraged me to pursue my calling. That calling has led me to teach and write, and to work outside the traditional Christian church structure. I have the freedom to follow where God leads.

Not all women have had that freedom however, so along with dedicating this book to Mary, I also dedicate it to all the women who are denied ministry due to church structures that refuse to allow women's rise in authority. I dedicate this to the women throughout the world who are still being beaten or shunned in a religion that proclaims "All are one in Christ" (Galatians 3:28) and that we are "to be a holy priesthood" (1 Peter 2:5).

I dedicate this to women who risk their lives doing the work of Jesus Christ. While *Broken For You* is a work of fiction, far too many women experience parts of it in their own lives. Through this work of fiction, I hope their stories will be told.

Acknowledgements....

IT TAKES A VILLAGE to create, and you would not be reading this book it if wasn't for the generosity of time and opinions of some very special people:

Susan who corrected my liturgical references and pointed out that this story might touch some very vulnerable places in the women who read it, reminding me to respect that pain.

Steve, Cathy and Talia who kept encouraging me even when other obligations meant they couldn't add their own personal opinion as often as we would have liked.

Julie, Mora and Sarah who asked questions as they read, helping me focus on what parts needed more attention.

Rena who routinely asked "Are you finished yet?" She was the push I needed because I was tired of giving her reasons why I hadn't yet published.

Marie, Heather and Maggie who promised to be my 'first sale', and kindly did not ask if I was finished.

Deb, Lynn and Jenn who edited with a smile on their face, no matter how often I kept misspelling the same words.

And my family. You have lived with this book for years, and are no doubt as happy as I am that *Broken For You* has finally taken flight.

CHAPTER ONE

RINGING IN THE DISTANCE got louder as Kendra Ward slowly came to consciousness. She slammed around her night table for her alarm clock before realizing it was her phone. "Yes" she uttered into the mic, not fully awake.

"Sorry, Kenny," the disembodied voice of Jack Hudson came on the other end, "we've got a fresh one."

Blinking rapidly, Kendra tried to make sense of why Jack would be calling her so early in the morning. She had just returned from a family gathering to bury one of her favourite aunts, and had another week to herself before she was expected to meet with him to go over some old cases.

Jack Hudson and Kendra Ward met in university where they both pursued degrees in Religious Studies, and after a brief fling realized they were better friends than lovers. Over the years they had been each others sounding board for personal and professional reasons. When the police force Jack worked for needed a specialist in religious hate crime, his friend Kendra was his first call. Kendra had finished her first degree then continued on to study Theology and become a priest, but after years working in small country churches, Kendra turned to writing and research, speaking to community events and lecturing at the university on hate crimes arising from religious misinformation and intolerance. Working with Jack had started out as consulting, then it became a side business when police forces throughout eastern Canada realized these were specialized crimes and they did not have the personnel to dedicate full time.

It worked well. Jack was the police officer with access to files and reports, while Kendra was the investigator with her own hand-picked team. They were an eclectic group, but each brought their own perspective to the crimes they examined. Her credentials as a crime scene investigator gave her an in with the local officials to help their communities stop similar crimes. Between writing, lecturing, researching and working scenes with Jack, she was extremely busy, which is why she was not happy to be on the phone at that early an hour.

"What? Already?" Kendra groaned, slowly coming to her senses. "It's what... 6 o'clock in the morning. Why can't the bad guys wait 'til noon?

Jack chuckled, "Good to see you can be funny at this hour."

"Who's being funny?"

"Up and at 'em, sleeping beauty. And be sure to grab coffee. The rest of the team has been called and they are already on their way. I let you sleep in while I made our arrangements, but we have to be at the airport in less than an hour. Dress warm."

"How long do you think this will take?" she yawned, as she pulled the blankets off her legs.

"Well... I wouldn't expect to see the inside of your house anytime this week. This one's quite messy, and given the Easter weekend, we're going to be hard pressed to get answers."

"I'll be right there, text me the information."

"Yeah, yeah..." was all she heard of Jack's fading voice as she pressed the button to end the call. Looking around her small bedroom Kendra sighed. She had just returned and wasn't looking forward to another flight this soon. Groaning one more time, she launched herself from the bed and moved downstairs to flick on the coffee maker, then opened the cupboards to see if anything looked appetizing. Her stomach rolled and she hoped that was because of hunger and not drinking too much while hopping time zones.

She returned to her bathroom and pulled her hair into an unruly mess on top of her head. After splashing cold water on her face, she pulled the rest of her clothing on, threw the essentials into her smaller suitcase and moved downstairs to collect her satchel and the largest travel mug for coffee she could find.

Traffic at that hour of the morning was easy, and before long Kendra found herself pulling into the airport's long term parking area. Jack was waiting by the gate as promised, ticket vouchers in hand. Swinging his arm over her shoulder, they went to security.

The flight was uneventful and they arrived just as Moncton, New Brunswick was starting to come alive. Another few hours in a rental car heading north to Dalhousie, and they were met by the rest of Kendra's team.

THE HOUSE BEFORE THEM looked like an old Edwardian farm house that had seen better days. Faint red paint was chipped away in some areas and the white trim was stained by the seasons. Trees towered over the driveway, casting shadows in all directions. Police tape was wrapped around the stairs to the front porch and out past the walkway to kept the already gathered crowd from entering the building.

"So what do we have?" Kendra asked, pulling gloves from her bag.

The first to greet her was her long time friend Theresa Goulet, an Indigenous woman who had spent most of her life trying to reclaim her history. Theresa had been adopted as a baby in what was now known as the Sixties Scoop; she had no idea where she belonged. After a suicide attempt someone suggested Theresa meet with a spiritual counsellor. That person turned out to be Kendra.

"The call came in yesterday," Theresa began, "one of the locals found the body and called us. It says here the caller was a Sister Margaret." She flipped through her notebook as they walked in through the front door, confirming the name. "A kid named Timmy was hovering around the door so she got curious. He seemed pretty scared by the whole thing."

"What did they say when they were questioned?"

"The kid's not talking and Sister Margaret is nowhere to be found."

"Lovely."

They walked in through the dark entryway and Theresa pointed towards a large room on their right behind French doors.

"A chapel?" she asked Theresa, and crossed herself.

"That's why we're here. Didn't Jack update you on the plane?"

"I fell asleep."

Nodding, Theresa led her into the small room and handed her a stack of pictures.

"For the love of God..." Kendra uttered, looking at the pictures of a naked woman laid out on the altar. Each picture showed the woman's body in greater detail focusing on the damage to her body. The victim's eyes were open as was her mouth. Holes went through the middle of both hands and ankles, and there were marks around her wrists and ankles that looked like rope burns. Faint traces of blood marked her left thigh, and there was a large stab wound on her right side where she had bled all over the white cloth on the table. The body had nothing to identify her except a large colourful cross around her neck.

"Stigmata?" she asked.

"Not sure," Jack answered behind her.

His voice surprised Kendra but she quickly turned back to the display in front of them, pictures in hand, "This table has been prepared."

"What?" Hugh MacLeod asked.

Hugh was the oldest member of the crew, a semi-retired police officer who complained he had nothing else to do besides work. At Kendra's request, he was placed on her team. She had no doubt his superiors were quite happy to have some place to put the curmudgeon. He was out of the way of any regular department, and close at hand so she could use him herself. Hugh might have been hard to get along with but he understood people and how even the best of humanity could turn to crime if they felt cornered. That insight was one of the biggest assets Kendra had to work with, and she was happy to put up with his foul temper.

Jack nodded and pointed around the table, drawing a confused look from Hugh. "Yup. The candle had been lit too."

The entire room had been set for a church service, seating twenty to thirty people. Chairs were stacked along the wall, and a small keyboard had been pushed to one side. A scattering of hymnals and prayer books were standing neatly in a small bookcase near the entrance. A large object hung from the wall with a purple cloth surrounding it, and Kendra immediately recognized it as a covered cross. Three movable kneelers lined the back wall behind the altar, each with identical prayer books on their small shelves.

"Kendra," Eli Avrams, the youngest member of her team, touched her elbow lightly as he held more pictures for her to see, "this was balled inside the victim's mouth."

She held one picture and looked at the printed words 'I Cor 14:34', then closed her eyes. "Oh Great."

Theresa and Jack looked at each other in silent communication and waited. They knew first hand how long Kendra had dealt with the bias against women in the church, and this new case hit a little close to home. "That's why I let her sleep," Jack finally whispered to an understanding Theresa.

Hugh seemed confused by the actions of the others and turned his attention to Kendra. "Kenny, what's going on?"

"This woman is a priest."

"How did you figure that? What do you think you're seeing?"

Kendra pointed around the room, "I'm seeing an altar set for mass, possibly from Maundy Thursday which was yesterday, but more likely for today's Good Friday service. I'm seeing a woman who might have been presiding here when most traditional churches will only accept men leading the worship services. I'm seeing a woman mutilated in the way Christ was on the cross. I'm seeing scripture that says women should remain silent shoved in her mouth to truly silence her. This is the embodiment of a religious controversy that has had the church arguing for centuries, and unless I miss my guess, I'm seeing a woman sexually assaulted as a reminder of what the killer thought of her."

"And you get all that looking at those pictures?" Hugh asked.

"This murder is covered in symbolism, Hugh," Kendra continued.

Hugh harrumphed, "Every murder is covered in symbolism."

Kendra nodded, "Yes, that's true, but this symbolism is jumping up and screaming it's intention. We're looking for someone or many someones, who are extremely angry with women in the priesthood and possibly even angry at the modern church itself."

"You can be that sure?"

"Yeah, I think I can."

CHAPTER TWO

SUCH A PRETTY PLACE, Kendra thought to herself as she and Jack drove up the hill that led to the outskirts of the town. Nestled in a small basin surrounded on all sides by water and hills, Dalhousie looked like the sleepy little Atlantic Canadian town often displayed by vacation pamphlets and tourist commercials. Everything suggested a slower pace of life where neighbour talked to neighbour, and three generations could live on the same street. How were they dealing with a murder in their town, she wondered. In the city something like that might go unnoticed until the evening news, but in a small town everyone probably knew about it before the police were called in, certainly before her own team of investigators arrived.

Pulling into the RCMP detachment, Jack looked over at Kendra. "We'll figure this out."

"Yeah..."

Once inside the detachment, Kendra and Jack starting putting the pieces together, mapping out how they would approach their investigation. The preliminary autopsy report had been awaiting them when they arrived, but they both knew the holiday weekend would put a crimp in how much they could use lab reports to find answers. Everything would be delayed.

"So what does it say?" Kendra asked. Jack had picked up the report first and had flipped through it before going back to the beginning for a focused read. The cover still said "Unknown Female Victim".

"This report confirm sexual assault. No signs of struggle and there were traces of benzodiazepines so my guess is Rohypnol or something in that family."

"Great," Kendra sighed. "What about the marks on her wrist and ankles, and the holes in her hands?"

Jack picked up the autopsy report and read further. "The wrists and ankles were definitely friction burns from rope. Can't tell if they were related to the sexual assault or not. If drugs were in her system then maybe she didn't need to be tied down."

"Mmm..." Nodding Kendra picked up the pictures of their victim's hands and feet. "Were they tied together or apart?"

"Excuse me?"

"Did the report say if her hands and feet were tied together or had they been tied to something else?"

"Doesn't say. What are you thinking?"

"Well if I were to guess, I'd say the ankles were tied together but the wrists weren't. See how the lines on the wrist go straight across? If the wrists were tied together, the marks on one or both arms would be at an angle in order to compensate for the path of the rope."

" True. If her legs were tied together, that kinda rules out being tied down then raped," Jack commented.

"What does it say about the rope?

"Ah... rough and low quality, and some fibers were still embedded in her skin. Something used on farms, standard stuff.

It does say the rope had mud embedded in it, which was transferred to the abrasions on her skin, so it was definitely either previously used or stored poorly. It was not new rope."

"And the hands?"

"That one seemed strange to the lab. Outside of the gaping hole there doesn't seem to be any other damage. It was done with something thick like spikes, and the holes were cauterized, which means whoever did this had the spikes heated before they pounded them into her hands."

Kendra closed her eyes for a minute to absorb the information. "Someone went to a lot of trouble for this woman's death. And the ankles?"

"Broken when the spike went through."

"My God..." Kendra said, shaking her head. "Any wood splinters on the body?"

Flipping through the pages Jack shook his head. "Um... no, not that I've seen, but this is just the first report and I can call them to make sure they swabbed her hands. Then we can see if there were any other particulates inside her wounds. It does say when they aligned the ankles with the rope burns, the holes that went through lined up as well, meaning whoever did this used only three spikes in total."

"Any idea what kind?"

"Again it says they were pretty basic. Straight shaft. Nothing marking them as extraordinary. I'm not sure how they were taken out since there are no other markings on the body. Wouldn't there be bruises or torn skin where they hammered them?"

"I guess that all depends on how and when. This is so gruesome and it's definitely a message. No wonder the locals called us in."

"Yeah, don't you love when we're the experts?" Jack said sarcastically.

"Tell me something, could she have been rolled over and the nails banged out the way they went in?" Hugh suggested.

"That's possible. But they would have had to use a secondary tool since the report says her hands and ankles have no extra marks." Kendra moved the pictures around, looking for something to explain the mystery of the spikes.

"Oh this is interesting," Jack continued reading, "it says her body had been wiped down with some kind of perfume, something spicy."

"Huh, that is interesting. What does it say about the stab wound on her side?"

"Ah, well I guess we are looking for a sword or large knife of some kind. The rest of the damage was bad, but the cut on her side was what killed her. The puncture went directly through her liver, lungs and nicked her heart, which accounts for the amount of blood on the table around her."

"So the stabbing was done at the crime scene, but the rest was done somewhere else?"

Jack nodded, "Yeah, that's what the report says."

"Okay," Kendra nodded, "we're looking for a second crime scene, some place secluded where the murder could rape her and perform this ritualistic mutilation. Considering he knew how to slice right to the heart and leave the hands unbroken, we're talking about someone who probably knows anatomy. Someone who is also well versed in Christian symbolism. Most people don't realize Jesus was sliced through the side just after he died, but this killer obviously does."

"Maybe they just got lucky."

"Perhaps, but given how everything else seems so methodical, let's just say for arguments sake that the final stabbing was intentional."

"I guess... So, what are we talking about here... medical student? Theology student? Sociopath?" Jack asked.

"Could be all three. Could be one person or more than one."

"Well the report says she wasn't gang raped so chances are it was one guy. He probably used a condom or a hard object because there was no sperm or foreign cells in the vagina."

"Any residue from the condom?"

"No evidence of lubricant."

"He really wanted her to suffer," Kendra acknowledged.

Jack looked at Kendra for a bit before speaking again. "You okay with all of this Kenny?"

"Which part," she snorted. "Death, mutilation or working on this murder when I should be on vacation?"

"All of it, but the last one I guess."

Kendra shrugged, "It's not like we picked this job to work with the nicer parts of humanity."

"True enough..."

CHAPTER THREE

"SO WHAT DO WE HAVE?" Kendra asked as she and Jack sat down for lunch with the rest of their team. They were in a small cafe sitting as far away from the locals as they could manage. Everyone seemed to know who they were, or at least why they were there. Small towns had some of the best information networks in the world, and a stranger was spotted in no time. That alone made Kendra wonder who their victim was and why no one was talking. That should have been the first thing they learned upon their arrival.

"I didn't get very far with identifying our victim," Yasmin began. She was the last of Kendra's team to arrive and began working the bystanders looking for potential witnesses. "People started acting strangely when I asked them questions, and most of them wouldn't answer at all. All I really got was the title "Mother". No last name, no known address before our crime scene. She was new to town which you know, should have raised suspicions, but they seemed to have accept her whole. They said this was her mission, but that's all I got."

"Let me have a go," Hugh cut Yasmin off. "I know how to get answers."

"I think in this time Jack or I should ask the questions." Kendra shot Jack a look and he nodded. Of the six people around the table only Jack and Kendra were actively religious.

"Why not me?" Hugh squawked in surprise.

Kendra took a few minutes to collect her thoughts as she looked at Hugh. As much as she knew he respected her, he really wasn't comfortable with her calling the shots and she knew she was going to have to walk gently. "Okay, here's the plain truth of the matter. Go talk to the townspeople for sure, but Jack and I will probably be the only ones to get information out of those we saw at the scene. We are dealing with religious people and religious people have their own language, kind of an inside speak. Religious people talk in symbolism and metaphors that are not shared by the general public."

"So what you're saying is that since you and Jack talk the talk, the rest of us are outsiders and useless," Hugh crossed his arms at the insult.

"Hugh, if this murder had happened at a Buddhist Temple or a Jewish Synagogue, the first thing I'd do would be to get people of that faith in here to act as consultants. It's hard to explain, but when you are part of a faith community, you become a sort of.... an extended family. We all share a common history and have shared stories, we talk in references and metaphors. Even our humour is very contextualized. Whoever murdered this woman knew a lot about Holy Week rituals, especially around the Eucharist. We are dealing with an insider, so we need people who have an inside knowledge to lead this case. You yourself just told me a short while ago that you didn't see everything at the crime scene that we did."

"And what... the rest of us are just supposed to hang around and gossip with the locals? What's the point of being here if we aren't going to do the job?" Hugh glared as he picked up his fork and started jabbing his food.

"No, please, I need you. That's too much for just two people. All I'm suggesting is that we pair up when we do interviews: religious and non-religious. The rest of the work is just like always, sweat and tears and fine tooth combs. You know that better than anyone."

"I've got to tell you, Kenny. I feel like my intelligence has been insulted," Hugh said, then he threw the fork he was holding onto the table.

"Look, it's like hockey," Jack intervened, taking Hugh's attention away from Kendra. The tension around the table was growing and it had to be defused.

"Like hockey? What the hell are you talking about?"

"You and me, we love the game, right? We know scores, we know players, we know the rules. Now, you talk to someone who doesn't know the rules, someone who's never held a stick before. We can't talk to them about hockey like we would each other. You know what I mean? We can't talk stats with someone who doesn't even know the difference between a power play and a penalty shot."

"That's bull Jack, and you know it. It doesn't take a genius to understand what the church is all about. All you have to do is turn on the TV and someone is preaching about hell and salvation, or some government official is taking an oath on a Bible they probably have never opened in their life, or some show is doing a funeral and everyone is dressed in black like they're supposed to be. You can't turn around without having religion thrown in your face, so don't tell me I can't possibly understand it."

"That's part of the problem. Everyone thinks they know it, but they don't. There is so much garbage being spread about the church you can't tell from one minute to the next what is real and what isn't. Take funerals: there is no rule about what you wear to a funeral, that's just what society thinks. The church doesn't have a dress code for that kind of thing."

"Hugh," Kendra took up the argument again, "this murder is saturated in symbolism that only someone truly inside would know. We have to approach this with a different set of eyes."

"I've worked as an investigator for a very long time, Kendra. I'm still training you how to do this job, for pete's sake. I know my way around a murder scene," Hugh glared at her.

"Yes, you do, we all know that. So can we put this discomfort to the side and work on it together?"

"Discomfort? Is that what you want to call it? You're saying that only you and Jack can properly figure this out and you want to call it 'discomfort'?" he practically spit at her.

Kendra tented her hands and leaned her forehead down.

"And what... now you're *praying* that I'll understand? Is that it?"

Jack crossed his arms and shook his head. "Give it a rest, old man. She's not praying, she trying to find the words to keep from telling you you're being an ass."

"I'm being an ass?" Hugh leaned over and glared directly at Jack. "You think you know what's going on? You go to the rink on Sunday mornings, you don't even go to church and I'm just supposed to believe you know something I don't?"

"Who says I don't go to church?" Jack asked him. "When we're working together, why do you think I take my lunch breaks at the same time every day? Wherever I'm working I try to find a church that does midday prayer and I drop in when I can."

"Midday prayer? What the hell is midday prayer."

"That's the point he's trying to make, Hugh," Kendra said gently. "Midday prayer is one of the regular services people attend when they worship. There's also morning and evening prayer, compline and vespers. I'm Anglican, and I attend mass regularly, too."

"Well I know you do, Kenny, you worked in the place for years," Hugh huffed.

"Jack does too," Theresa spoke up quietly. "He's got a cross that he wears around his neck, and he did that kneeling thing when first got to the chapel this morning."

"It's called genuflecting, and my kind of cross is called a crucifix."

"What's the difference?" Yasmin looked confused.

"A cross is empty. A crucifix has the body of Christ."

"So?" Hugh still didn't understanding the difference.

Kendra added gently, "Hugh, a cross is worn by Protestants and Orthodox to recognizes Easter morning, while a crucifix is worn by Catholics to remember the sacrifice of Christ on the cross on Good Friday."

"Seriously?" Eli finally spoke up. "There's different jewelry depending on what church you belong to?"

"Sort of," Kendra smiled at him. "It's not a perfect distinction. I've seen Protestants wear the crucifix and Catholics wear nothing, but there is a standard. Look Hugh," returning her attention to him, "we aren't talking about fashion and entertainment, we're talking about more than 2000 years of tradition and battling out differences of opinion until most people agreed. Neither of us can brief you enough for you to catch everything, it would take too long. We are going to handle interviews by going in pairs. Jack and I will team with anyone else. It's the fastest way we can do this."

"Fine Kendra," Hugh glared at her as he stood up, "but know this, you just drew a line right through this team and you can't take it back."

Kendra's mouth hung open as Hugh left the table and marched out of the room. She had never seen Hugh as angry as he was at this moment.

"That old bastard!" Jack muttered, before taking a drink from the coffee in front of him.

"How did we get to this point?" Kendra asked no one in particular.

"Oh, just let the old guy blow it off. He does this sometimes." Jack said without turning towards her. "I've seen him try to throw his weight around."

"I didn't try to draw a line through this team."

"And you didn't," Theresa said, patting her arm. "I'll give him a minute and then go and knock some sense into him. The old goat thinks he knows everything and he doesn't like being reminded that other people know things too."

Kendra put her free hand over her eyes for a few seconds, than shook her head and rolled her shoulders. "Yeah, thanks..."

Shaking off the frustration, Kendra picked the pictures up from the open file in front of her. "Hmmm, interesting... Jack, look at this," she said, holding up a closer picture of the paten and chalice that had been placed in front of the body.

Yasmin looked with Eli at the picture. "What are you seeing?" she asked, "all I see is a plate and fancy cup."

Jack pointed to the chalice, "See, the cup is ready for someone to drink. If this table had been prepared for a service, the cup would have had a flat thing on top of it. It's called... um..."

"Pall," Kendra supplied.

"Yeah, right. It's a pall, and it has a folded cloth napkin inside called the purificator. When someone hasn't started the Eucharist part of the service, the chalice is covered. So whoever set this up was intending it to be used right away. There isn't even a veil over it. And see, the cross is facing outwards, away from where the congregation would see it."

"So you think someone planned on drinking from it?" Theresa asked.

"That or someone was ready to put something in."

"Put something in...." Kendra started thinking. "Oh, why didn't I see this. Look at the position of the blood on the table cloth."

"Blood and body," Jack rolled his eyes in realization. "She was the sacrifice."

"Someone care to explain that?" Yasmin asked.

'Hmm," Jack started, "basically, the night before Christ died, he had supper with all his friends and took the bread and said that was his body, and he gave a piece to everyone to eat. He told them he wanted them to always do that and remember him when they ate. Then he lifted a cup filled with wine and said that was his blood that he would shed for everyone to wipe away their sins, and that when they drank wine, they were part of his promise to change the world."

"Sounds a little cannibalistic to me," Theresa replied.

"That's what the Ancient Romans thought too," Kendra offered as she continued flipping through the pictures. "So when Rome burned, it didn't take Emperor Nero long to convince everyone that it was the Christian's fault. We were hunted on and off for 200 years after that."

"Charming," Theresa muttered.

"I wonder....," Kendra thought out loud. "I wonder if the placement is telling. Our victim is laid out like she was on a cross, but her body is not on the plate and her blood never made it to the cup. Do you think this could be someone who knew how to lay the table? Eli can you get a list of all of the seminaries and divinity halls in this part of country. Usually graduates don't go very far. Let's see who we can find that might have access to our crime scene. Maybe we'll get lucky and the victim will be a graduate as well."

"That's making the assumption that our killer put the body like this intentionally," Eli countered.

"True, but given the great care to detail in the mutilation of the victim's body, it's as good a place as any to start. The fact that she was placed like this on the night between Maundy Thursday and Good Friday just reinforces that everything about this murder was intentional and meant to send a message."

"Because..." Yasmin asked, needing more explanation.

"Maundy Thursday is when Jesus had his last supper with his friends, and then he went outside the city walls to a nearby park to pray. He was arrested then and his trial, torture and death happened the next day, Good Friday. The victim had her last meal with her friends, then faced her torture while everyone else was asleep."

Yasmin crossed her arms and looked at the others around the table, "So let me get this straight, this death is patterned after the whole Maundy Thursday/Good Friday thing? All this symbolism you guys see, is pointing to who you think did it? I gotta say Kendra, I'm with Hugh. I'm not convinced."

"I'm not either," Kendra assured her, "but right now it's all we really have to go on. At least this way we can figure out who it isn't. We might be dealing with someone highly educated or someone with severe mental issues. The church certainly attracts both."

CHAPTER FOUR

THERESA FOUND HUGH pacing the sidewalk outside the eatery.

"Blown through your temper yet?" she asked, stopping a few feet away and crossing her arms.

Grumbling, he looked at her, "What do you want?"

"I want to know if you've pulled your head out."

Hugh made a few more grunting sounds, the looked up to the sky. "I just don't like being told I'm stupid," he finally admitted.

Shaking her head, Theresa moved closer. "She wasn't doing that and you know it. Look, I was around all that church business growing up and I don't know even a fraction of what they know. Those two have degrees in this stuff. What do you and I have, sitting in cold buildings being talked at and bored to death? She wants to get this solved and us home as soon as she can. Can't you give her that one?"

"You seen one murder, you've seen them all," Hugh grumbled again.

Theresa snorted.

"They get anything?"

"Yeah, lots of talk about sacrifice and body placement on the table. She sent Eli to get the list of all schools in this part of the country that teach that stuff. Maybe we'll get luck."

"Huh.... I could a told them to start there... but what do I know..."

Theresa smiled, he was coming around. "Yeah, and when you stop feeling sorry for yourself Kendra has a job for you."

YASMIN AND JACK DROVE down the long drive towards the old building, and parked beside the crime tape. Bouquets of flowers were already in display around the fence, right up to the crime scene tape.

"I always find that creepy," she said before getting out of the car.

"What?"

"The flowers and teddy bears and candles. I mean where were these people when the victim was alive? Were they anywhere around here? Were they able to save her and didn't do anything? You know what I'm saying... sometimes it looks like people enjoy death so they can show off."

"Yeah, there's something to that," Jack agreed.

"You don't think I'm evil for thinking that?"

Jack smiled, "Nope. I'm always suspicious of these people gathering and leaving stuff at the crime scene. Too many times the killer is among them wanting to see everyone's reaction."

"Good point."

"Okay, what ground did you cover before?"

"Not much. As soon as they saw my notebook, they clammed up. I couldn't get very far with my questions. I'm not even sure she worked here."

"Kendra thinks she was from this place, and I have a hunch she's right."

"Why?"

"Because the murderer took too much trouble displaying the body. Usually that only happens when the location of the crime is really significant to either the victim or the murderer. Besides if people know her as 'Mother' it probably was religious. Guys are known as brother or father, and this murder was called in by a 'Sister' Margaret."

"Makes sense," Yasmin shrugged.

Together, they walked to the crowd gathered around the impromptu memorial and started showing the best picture they had of their victim's face. Some didn't recognize her, but others seemed to react. Jack looked over the top of one woman at Yasmin, and shrugged. The woman didn't speak at all. The only indication that she understood the question was her glance over at the memorial to a recently placed picture of their victim, alive and happy, and then moved on in silence.

"What do you think?" Yasmin asked when they were close enough to whisper.

"When you said no one talked to you, I thought you meant they just weren't forthcoming. I didn't realize they really didn't talk to you."

"It was weird, I gotta tell you. They all looked sad but there's no sound, not even crying."

"Okay," Jack said as he picked up one picture of their victim, then placed his hand on Yasmin's lower back as he led them away from the people milling around the memorial. "Let me think about this for a minute."

"Don't some of these places keep silent? I think I read about that once."

"Sometimes different monasteries do, and they all have rules that change with the season and time of day."

"So how do we know which is which?"

"I.. I'm.... to tell you the truth, this is where it gets really complicated. There's overall traditions like Benedictine and Trappist and others, that have certain rules that people seem to like. But then there's the tradition of a place itself that modifies those rules. For all I know, they could be making this up as they go along and only they know what they're doing."

"Great... " Yasmin muttered as she followed behind him.

They turned and made their way back to the red house. Just as they were about to climb the stairs, Jack stopped. "Has the scene been cleared?"

"I don't think so. Why don't you call Hugh and see if he heard anything."

Jack shook his head, "I've got a better idea, why don't you call Hugh."

"Me? Why me?"

"Because you're on his side of this 'divide line', so he's more likely to talk to you than me at the moment." Jack made quotation marks with his fingers.

Yasmin shook her head while she took out her phone. "That's all stupid anyway," she said as she waited for Hugh to pick up the other end. "What am I supposed to ask him?"

"Just see how much of the crime scene did they release...."

"Hi Hugh," she held up her hand to silence Jack as her call was answered. "I'm out here at the site and I'm wondering how much of this tape we can take down. Ah-huh.... yeah... okay, but not the house itself. Thanks."

"Is he still grumpy."

"Yeah, I think that's safe to say," she said as she pocked her phone.

"It's a ridiculous power struggle. Kendra was just covering all the bases."

"Maybe, but I can understand where Hugh's coming from."

"Then could you explain it to me, because I'm not getting it," Jack stopped on the front stairs of the building and turned to look at her, hand on his hips.

Yasmin pulled at the crimes scene tape, trying to collect her thoughts. "Well... the way it came across made it sound like you guys were superior to us simply because you know this church stuff and we don't."

"I don't get that. I don't think I'm better, and I'm know for sure Kendra doesn't think that way. Look, just because we have faith in God doesn't make us think we're chosen or special or anything like that. It's just what makes sense to us. It feels good at the end of a long day to get down on my knees and pray. It's just nice knowing I've always got someone with me, no matter what I'm doing. Someone I can talk to and who will understand, no questions asked."

"You're making this sound like God is a real person."

"He is to me."

Theresa considered what Jack said as they entered the building, gathering all the yellow tape as they went. Then she watched him place the tape to the front door to cut off access just outside the house. Before they entered the small chapel Theresa watched Jack wet his fingers in a little bowl on the side of the wall and mark an X on his forehead.

"I didn't see that before, what is that?" she asked, pointing to the decorative bowl hanging on the wall.

"Huh?" Jack turned to look where she was pointing. "Oh, that's a holy water font. See the chipped white thing in the chapel?" He pointed to a large plaster sculpture against the back wall, that looked like a gigantic cup. "That's the primary font, and when the water is blessed there, they bring a little bit out here so people can cross themselves before they enter the chapel."

"So you just dip your fingers and touch your head?"

"Yes and no. Yes that's what you do, but it's baptismal water, so every time you do it you're reconfirming your baptism."

"Okay. And that crossing thing you do, I saw you and Kendra do it."

"Everyone has their own style. I genuflect and cross myself with the water, Kendra just crosses herself, and some people don't do anything. They just walk into the chapel and take a deep breath."

"So that all means something different too? Like the cross necklace thing?"

"Nah, it's just personal choice. It probably says a lot about how we were raised, but it doesn't really say anything about what we believe."

"I gotta tell you, Jack, I'm not clear on what is important and what is just personal style."

"It takes awhile, and you have to know there are other ways to do things, otherwise you just assume what you do is what everyone should do. That's when we get into trouble. Every war that was ever fought over religion is someone trying to force others to do things their way. It never works in the end, and a lot of people are dead."

ACROSS THE HALL FROM the chapel was a small library that looked well used. Two mis-matched, overstuffed armchairs were placed in front of the window. Books were piled to overflowing on the home-make shelves, and the one side table in the room was covered by magazines.

"What do you think?" Yasmin asked Jack as they took a look around. "These books tell you anything?"

"Some. Not much, but I don't read as much of this stuff as I used to. Kendra could tell us what they believe here based on who wrote these books."

"It is really that complicated?" Theresa asked.

"Ah yup, I'm afraid so. You could have a whole street full of bookstores, and every store would have different books trying to convince you why they were right and everyone else was wrong. The good news is this tells us something about the people here. The bad news is unless you know what you're looking at, you're hopelessly lost."

Yasmin rolled her eyes and shook her head as they moved out of the room. Further into the house they saw a dining area and kitchen, with two small rooms in the back. One was a laundry room with a large chest freezer and a full pantry. The second room had cupboards and shelves full of books, wine, small cloths, candles and bottles of liquid. "Sacristy", Jack said before moving on. "We'll come back to that."

Upstairs they found bedrooms and bathrooms. Three of the bedrooms looked the same with mismatched twin beds, desks, dressers and night tables. The last bedroom contained a desk facing the door. The walls were decorated with posters, inspirational sayings and a collage of pictures.

"Success!" Jack declared when they walked in. He pointed to a computer drawn picture that seemed like a map.

"About time. I was wondering if we would ever find an office in this place." Yasmin took the map off the wall and looked at the various buildings. The chapel and library were well marked. There appeared to be two other buildings that were strictly residential, and a fourth building was marked 'office'. "I guess this isn't the real office after all."

"This reminds me of the nun's office when I was a kid in school," Jack said as they entered the final building on their map.

"Good times?"

"Nope."

"Then why do you still go to church?"

"My faith is in God. Being Catholic is just how I show it. Look at this," he held up a picture.

"Joan?" she read the name under the picture. "At least we now we can confirm her name."

"Maybe," Jack replied pulling the picture out of it's frame and looking for any writing on the back.

"Why maybe, her name is right under her picture?"

"Yeah, but that doesn't mean it was her real name. More than likely that's her professional name. See on the back is says 'Pope'?"

"So she's Joan Pope?"

"Maybe."

Yasmin stood back and looked at Jack. "I gotta tell you, this church thing is making no sense to me. Nothing is what it looks like and everything has hidden meanings or aliases or movements like a secret handshake. How are we ever going to know what's real?"

"We just have to keep looking and hope it all comes together."

CHAPTER FIVE

LATER THAT AFTERNOON Hugh came quietly back into their shared office at the RCMP detachment and sat down. Kendra looked up to see him slip into a seat, and smiled to herself. She was glad he had returned.

Sighing heavily, Hugh flipped through a book he had brought with him, then threw it down on the desk. "I just.... I just feel so frustrated," he announced.

"Hugh?" Kendra asked softly, looking at Theresa.

Hugh leaned forward on the table, first making sure it was only the three of them. "I just feel I'm not able to work this case, and I don't like that feeling."

"Why do you feel that?" she asked gently.

Hugh moved his hands back and forth in an attempt to find the words, then he roughly got out of his chair and shoved it into his desk.

"I looked at the pictures of that woman's body this morning, and saw only a fraction of what I was supposed to see. I've been to more than my fair share of crime scenes over the years, and some of those were in churches. Did I mess up on those too?"

"I don't know, but if I was to guess, I'd say if you solved those murders, you did everything you could."

"Yeah, we did. But could I have done more?"

"Hey, Hugh, I've been around the block a few times myself, and I've seen some things I wish I could erase from my memory. I can tell you this one's different. This one's a statement," Kendra assured him.

Hugh huffed, "All murders are a statement. It's just the level of sophistication in this one. I'm so out of my league, and I owe you apology for earlier, Kenny."

"Thank you, Hugh."

"Look, I don't want to say this with the others around, and if you repeat this I'm going to deny it, but I feel like a rookie. Like this is my first case and I'm getting everything wrong. I even picked this up at the drug store around the corner, and I don't know the first thing about it."

Theresa reached over and picked up the pristine new Bible from Hugh's hand. "What were you looking up?"

"That note shoved into her mouth. I'm guessing it's some reference, but I haven't had a Bible in my hands since I was a kid. I don't know anything." Hugh clasped and unclasped his fist, showing how deeply his sense of frustration truly ran.

Theresa passed the book to Kendra who opened it to the first book of Corinthians, at the 14th chapter, verse 34, then passed it to Hugh to read. "*Let your women keep silence in the churches: for it is not permitted unto them to speak; but they are commanded to be under obedience, as also saith the law. And if they will learn anything, let them ask their husbands at home: for it is a shame for women to speak in the church.*"

When he was finished reading, Kendra sighed. "It's one of those more frequently used arguments for women not being priests. People are always taking it out of context and forget that this was a response to a problem happening in Corinth at the time, not a rule for everyone in the Christian community to follow."

"How can you be part of something that tells you to be quiet in public. And is goes on to say ask your husbands if you want to know something? How many domestic abuse cases have we had where the husband thinks it's his right to keep his wife silent and dependent? I gotta say, Kenny, you are far too intelligent a woman to believe this. Aren't you?"

"That's why you have to study this book, Hugh, and not just read things as if they were written in today's world. Paul is the name of the person who wrote that, and he was a first century Hebrew man. It's almost comical because he tells women to be silent here, and then at the end of his letters he thanks a lot of women by name for all the work they are doing for the church. At the end of that letter he names Priscilla, one of the most referenced women in the New Testament, and salutes her and her husband for the church in their home. His letter to the Romans thanks nine different women for their leadership, and calls Phoebe a deacon and Junia an apostle. Priscilla is there too, and Phoebe was in Corinth and sent to Rome as his emissary, so he obviously had no problem working with women. But something was happening in Corinth at the time that he wanted to fix. We don't have the problem, just his answer. He was writing at a time when most girls and boys weren't taught to read and write, and he didn't want women interrupting to ask questions. It wasn't even about women, this whole passage is about how to worship peacefully without distraction. Those things that didn't make sense needed to be talked about at a later time, not in the middle of worship. But that's the problem with taking a few lines out of the Bible and saying it is against women. No... the truth was the rich women of the day, the women who could read and write, were the ones who kept Paul and the other followers fed and clothed, and held church services in their homes. Priscilla was one of them, so was Mary Magdalene for Jesus. Claudia is named. I can't remember who else, but women were part of Paul's ministry, so he must have been responding to something very specific that was happening in Corinth.

"How do you keep that all straight?" Theresa asked.

Kendra shrugged, "Read. There's a 2000 year history of working with this stuff. You can go to church, sit in the pew, do what you're told, and it'll never really mean anything. Or you can worship, read about it, go to lectures and spend time around other people who are struggling with the same questions. You know... put work into it."

"Seems a lot of hassle for nothing."

"And sometimes it feels that way," Kendra sighed.

Hugh looked surprised at her admission.

"Then why bother?"

"Mmm... because it means something to me. It makes me feel I'm part of something larger. I like the people. I like the efforts made by believers to improve the world around them. I don't have to agree with everything, none of us do. But the basics make sense. I really love wresting with this intellectually. You know the central focus of the Christian faith really hasn't changed in 2000 years. Love, serve others, protect and provide for the vulnerable, know there's something waiting for you when this life is over. That's all the same. It's only the community of thought and practice that have changed generation after generation. And when you happen upon something written in the twelfth century by a person struggling with the same issues you are, and when you see how they handled it, it might help provide answers. Besides I had help. My aunt specialized in this and taught at a university. I learned a lot from her."

Theresa titled her head and smiled sadly, "The aunt who just died?"

"Yeah..."

"We got something, Kendra," Yasmin announced bursting into the room, effectively bringing the private conversation between Kendra and Hugh to a close.

"Did you confirm the victim's name?"

"Maybe," Jack offered.

"Maybe? What's maybe?" Hugh look back and forth between the two.

"Her name is Joan," Yasmin began.

"Well, she calls herself Joan," Jack countered.

"Joan, as in Joan of Arc?" Hugh asked.

"Nope, as in Pope Joan."

"Oh boy...." Kendra shook her head.

"Does that mean something to you?" Theresa asked.

"Yes and no. Pope Joan is believed to be the only female Pope the Catholic church has ever had. She lived in the 700's, and legend says she dressed like a man, and lived like a man, and eventually she was elected Pope. She's pretty much been erased from the memory of the Catholic Church, but there are lots of references to her and a whole lot of questions."

"She was a legend, Hugh" Jack offered.

"Perhaps," Kendra countered. "I know there's no hard proof, but the circumstantial evidence is quite compelling."

"There's no proof, Ken," Jack reiterated.

"I thought you Christians agreed on everything," Theresa teased

"Hardly," Kendra snorted, then turned back to Jack. "Given the era, proof would be hard to come by. Besides, our modern concept of substantiated evidence can hardly be applied to the Middle Ages when everything was different. The very fact that writer after writer made reference to her means someone had to exist who came up through the academic ranks by disguising herself as a male, and was ultimately elected Pope. It's not hard to believe given the stories of the mystics at the time. Just because the church patriarchy wants to pretend they weren't duped doesn't mean it didn't happen."

"Can we deal with the woman murdered in the 21st century, and then we'll get around to the one murdered in the 8th century," Jack scoffed.

"Murdered?" Theresa tone changed from teasing to surprised.

Jack nodded, "Yeah, the story goes that Joan gave birth in the middle of the street, and as soon as the Cardinals and Bishops around her realized she was a woman, they stoned her to death and killed her new son."

"Ugh... why do you want to be part of something that hates women? Especially you, Kendra?" Yasmin looked disgusted.

"Yasmin, that would take a very long conversation, and one we don't have time for at the moment. Suffice it to say, not everyone in the church hates women, and the patriarchal church has been accused of a lot over the years, but not all of it is true." Turning to Jack she asked, "What else do we have for identification of our victim?"

"She calls herself 'Joan', but there wasn't anything else in the office of a personal nature. No business cards, phone bills, diplomas. We did find this, however. Letterhead that says '*Bet-Neshar*'. Ah House of the Vultures."

"Excuse me?" Kendra looked at him.

"It's Hebrew. *Bet* means house, and *Neshar* is sometimes translated as eagle, but more accurately a vulture."

"Do you think that means anything?"

"Well, that species of bird lives in a group, called a 'wake' or a 'committee', and members are free to come and go as they please. I'll make a call and see if the name is registered," Jack said stepping away from the table to make a phone call.

"Kendra, do you think that's the kind of group this Joan was running?" Theresa asked.

"Perhaps. We should ask the locals what they know and be a little more direct this time. A town this size usually talks about anything new. Maybe it's an intentional community, you know groups of people who come together for a project or communal living. Small towns like this would attract groups like that, especially artistic groups or people who want to work on the land or start a new business. There's a pier just down the street. Let's see what kind of ships they get. Maybe this is a lesser known travel destination."

"Got it, Kendra," Jack interrupted as he returned, "our 'Pope Joan' has the building listed as her primary address, but her secondary address is a village about two hours from here. And according to their records, her real name is Tricia Steward."

"Okay, let's see who knows her by the name Joan and Tricia. She's in Dalhousie for a reason, let's figure it out."

"More here," Jack spoke again, scrolling through the texts on his phone. "Tox is back. Nothing new on drugs in her system. Rope was generic, so there's nothing to go on there. The holes in her hands and ankles were cauterized, but they had traces of down."

"Down? Like feather pillows?"

"She was tied to pillows?" Kendra looked up at Jack. "I would have thought something hard, but that certainly explains the lack of bruising."

"Okay everyone, we need to shut this down for tonight." Hugh spoke up. "It's been a long day for everyone and we need to start fresh tomorrow. First thing in the morning, Yasmin find Eli, and look for anything you can find on Tricia Steward. Where she went to school, when she graduated, if she was married, you know the drill. Theresa make nice with the locals and see if people will talk. Kenny and I are going on a road trip."

"And me?" Jack asked with a slight smirk, amused by Hugh's need to exert authority.

"You, you start putting this stuff together and see if that encyclopedia you have for a brain can see other connections. So far you seem to be hitting all the highlights with our local Pope."

"You know," Kendra started, "if Tricia patterned herself after Pope Joan, she might have had a lover who helped her get where she wanted to go. The original wouldn't have gotten as far as she did without help."

"And where there's a secret lover, there are more secrets." Hugh looked at everyone.

Theresa nodded in agreement, and added her own thoughts, "With the way the body was handled, I'm starting to think the killer couldn't make up his mind if he loved her or hated her."

"Theresa, you might be on to something."

CHAPTER SIX

"HERE WE ARE," HUGH announced needlessly as they pulled into the driveway of Tricia Steward's home late the next morning. They had driven in silence, both lost in their own thoughts.

"Can I help you?" a surprised older woman asked, coming around the corner.

"Do you live here?" Kendra asked her.

"No, I live over there," she pointed to the house across the street. "But Tricia's not home. I look after her cat when she's away. I do it regularly, don't you know. She spends so much time at that church place of hers now, I don't know why she even bothers keeping a house. But I suppose, people like that need to have their house and their work far apart. Leads to a normal life, I guess. I was just closing up and going home. I need to get back for my shows, don't you know," she smiled, and Kendra smiled along with her.

"Ms.?" Kendra began.

"Miss... Miss Chapman. I'm the neighbour. I've lived here for years and years. I'm kind of the neighbourhood watch, if you know what I mean."

"Yes, I do. Miss Chapman, my name is Kendra Ward, and this is Hugh McLeod. We're working with the RCMP. We need to ask you some questions about Tricia Steward, if you don't mind. But first, would you mind opening the door so we could look around?"

"Is Tricia in some kind of trouble, dear?"

"Tricia was murdered last night, Miss Chapman. We're doing everything we can to find her killer. You could be an enormous help."

"Tricia... " Miss Chapman put her hand over her heart, and Kendra moved in closer to grab the woman in case she started to teeter. "I'm okay, but Tricia... she was such a good neighbour. Always so kind. She'd bring people home for dinner if they needed food. She'd never let them stay. She had that church place full of beds, but sometimes people just needed a body to talk to. I'd see her lights on for hours into the night."

"Did she have anyone around recently? Anyone who struck you as being a threat to her?"

"Who? Oh, it's hard to say. She'd pick up people off the streets or have the town's loose women for tea. Everyone was welcome in her house. She always has ice cream or some kind of treat for the children around here. She has a large bin of toys just outside her back door so they could come and borrow anything they needed to play. And they always brought them back, of course. That was the deal: borrow what you need, but return it for someone else to use. She was just one of those people who always helped others. She was a priest, don't you know. She didn't work in a real church and I never had the whole story, but she seemed to really like people."

"Did Tricia have a husband or boyfriend that you knew of?"

"No husband. No children. No family, I don't think. At least she never visited anyone out of town and she never had people staying with her. I seen her with a man from time to time, but I can't tell you what was going on. Some had those collars on their shirts, you know the ones that said they were priests too, but not every one. And there weren't that many, I want to just say that. She didn't have men over a lot. She wasn't that kind of girl."

"Was there anything recently that upset her?" Hugh asked.

"No.... not that I know of. She didn't really talk about her life that much. She'd invite me for tea and she'd be so good to listen to me. Come to think of it, all she ever did was listen to me... she was kind a special that way, don't you know? She always made me feel like I was the only one in the room that mattered. Others said the same thing. She'd just listen."

"Do you mind letting us in, Miss Chapman?"

"Oh... oh, my. I'm sorry. This has got me all turned around. Yes dear, I'll let you in. Do you need me to stay?"

"Thank you, but it would be better if we did this without anyone around. I hope you understand."

"Yes... yes, of course. I've got to tell the girls what happened. The neighbours will want to know. Should I tell them you'll be around to speak with everyone?"

Kendra smiled at the older woman, "Yes, that would be helpful, thank you."

Once they were inside and Miss Chapman was halfway across the street, Hugh finally spoke. "Nothing so helpful to the police than a neighbourhood busy-body who likes to talk."

"Be nice, Hugh. She was obviously upset by this."

Hugh grumbled but didn't say anything further. There had been no signs of struggle, nothing seemed out of place or overly messy. It looked like the home of a single woman who spent more time at work than she did in her private space. Bookshelves covered one wall of the main room, and disappeared into a dining area that had been turned into an office. A small table in the kitchen seemed the only space dedicated to eating. Off to one side of the tiny bungalow, they found a bedroom and bathroom. Bookshelves lined the hallway and much of the second bedroom as well. Downstairs they found a large storage room with rows of boxes labeled 'mugs,' 'clothing: men,' 'books,' 'personal items' and more. There seemed to be a collection of items for any need. A simple laundry room was the only other area in the basement.

"There doesn't seem to be room for anyone else in this house," Hugh stated the obvious.

"Or her life, it would seem," Kendra agreed.

Outside, Kendra found the large toy box just as Miss Chapman had said she would. The small backyard was poorly tended, in stark contrast with the rest of the house. Empty pots and bags of soil were lined against the fence, suggesting a project that had never begun.

Going back inside house, Kendra knew there wasn't much more they could find. The few photos that were on display didn't have any identification or listing of names on their back, and there were no personal letters in the basket by the front door.

"Kendra," Hugh called as he came out of the bedroom.

"Yes?"

"We've got a laptop, two Diplomas, and this." He handed her a book and awaited her reaction.

Kendra looked at the title of the book and her face softened. She didn't look up as she caressed the cover. "Where did you find this?"

"It was on her beside table. It's signed."

"She knew Aunt Mary," Kendra said in wonder.

"I remember that time I met her," Hugh began. "It was that reception you dragged me to years ago. I wasn't the least bit interested in her topic, but we got to chatting anyway. Mary was quite the gal. I don't think I've ever seen anyone as enthusiastic about what she believed as Mary. She'd get her hands going and her smile was large, and before you knew it, you couldn't help be caught up in her excitement. She was contagious."

Kendra smiled at the memory, "She was something, alright. She never left the Roman Church, but she was completely convinced they were mistaken in their attitude toward women. This book Tricia kept on her bedside table, was my aunt's final work. It was her masterpiece, putting together over two decades of research. I'm a little stunned by the fact this woman was a student of my aunt's. Mind you, it's just one more piece of the puzzle that explains who Tricia was. Who else was a student with Tricia, I wonder?"

"Let's grab some of this stuff and get back to the office and see what the others have found. You can call them and tell them about this information while I drive."

Kendra nodded, and they left the house together. After a quick knock on Miss Chapman's door to tell her she could lock up the house and assuring her they would return to talk to the neighbours if necessary, they returned to Dalhousie.

"HUGH, KENDRA," ELI greeted them excitedly when they returned. "We've done quite a bit of research on Tricia Steward. Both parents are deceased. One brother, but it seems they haven't spoken in years. I looked up his blog, and he is a militant atheist, so that might explain the estrangement. She's quite educated. She has a Bachelor Degree, as well as a M.A., and was working on a Ph.D."

"That would match the framed diplomas I found," Hugh noted.

"Miss Chapman said she was a priest, but an M.A. is not the qualifying degree. Any hint of an M.Div. anywhere?" Kendra asked.

"Nope. Her Ph.D. director was Dr. Mary Schuller, recently deceased. That might mean something."

"Mary Schuller?" Jack smiled. "Now that's a name I know well."

Kendra nodded, "Okay everyone, in the spirit of full disclosure, Dr. Mary Schuller was my aunt."

Eli looked up in surprised, "Your aunt, the one who just died?"

"Yes."

"Oh Kendra, I'm sorry. I didn't make the connection."

Kendra smiled at the younger man, "That's okay."

"She was a fine lady," Jack shook his head at the memories, "smart as a whip and befuddled by the simplest things. Kendra, is this too much?"

Kendra looked at Jack in confusion. "What? Because my aunt was her teacher? I didn't know Tricia at all."

"No, I mean you and your Aunt Mary were close. You worked with her as a researcher when you were in school, and you helped with her lectures sometimes. Women in ministry is personal to you, and seeing someone killed for having the same attitudes about the church as Mary... well... it's not been that long since Mary, you know. Some things trigger when we least expect it."

Kendra smiled sadly then reached out to squeeze his hand. "Thanks, Jack, but I'm fine. I can separate personal and professional. I'll let you know if it gets too much."

"Kendra," Hugh started again, "did the inscription in the book mean anything?"

Kendra looked a bit flustered. Hugh had shown her the book but she hadn't actually looked inside. Opening it for the first time, Kendra read "To my favourite student. I have every confidence you will take these ideas and run with them. Yours always, Mary."

"Well, they were obviously close, too. What's the book about, Kendra?" Theresa asked.

"Mary spent a lifetime researching how women in the early church and into the Middle Ages were priests and leaders. She spend a lot of time in the Roman catacombs, and throughout Italy. She argued the the church would always be weak as long as it denied 50% of its population. Obviously our Tricia Steward agreed and wasn't prepared to wait for the church to come around. Mary would be devastated to know a student of hers died for this."

"We still don't know that was the reason, Kendra," Hugh said gently.

"She never wanted to be a priest, you know," Kendra said to no one in particular. "Mary always believed everyone should have the right to preside over the sacraments. She thought people should be educated in their faith, but elitism had no business in a community that professed to follow Christ's lifestyle."

"Kendra...."

"I'm alright, Jack, I'm just thinking we are slightly off the mark. Our Tricia Steward chose her name carefully, didn't attempt to get the qualifications of traditional priests, lead a community with no recognized structure.... she patterned her ministry after Christ himself. Perhaps she was killed for those choices."

"So you thinking this isn't a hate crime after all?" Hugh asked.

"No, it's definitely a hate crime, but perhaps the hate was directed at Tricia the person rather than what she represented."

"That would kinda make sense, especially since she was tied to pillows. Do you think this was an affair that went wrong?" Theresa asked. "Pillows are for beds, and beds mean sex for most people."

"Maybe. She was raped, but why she was raped is an open question. I still think the best shot we have is looking at former students as well as *Bet-Neshar* itself. Eli, anyone in the student body or faculty that presents a question mark needs to be investigated. Look up both Tricia Steward and Dr. Mary Schuller, and see what you can find. Theresa, could you and Hugh go back to the *Bet-Neshar* and start banging on doors. It's almost dinner time now, so people will be ending their day."

"Kendra," Hugh asked in surprise, "didn't you say we should pair up churched and unchurched?"

"We're way beyond looking for symbolism at every turn. This murder needs to be solved, and Christian symbolism is only part of the equation. Where did the killer rape and mutilate our victim? When would he have had the opportunity? Motive is only a small part of this, and we're well on our way to understanding what is behind this. Now I need to know where this could have happened."

CHAPTER SEVEN

"YOU READY TO ROLL?" Jack asked quietly after everyone left, waiting as he watched her touch the book they had found in Tricia's home.

"Did you know I helped her edit this?" she said to him, not really expecting an answer. "It was years ago when she first started writing it. She wanted to know if it made sense, if the language was clear. She was always worried that she talked above people's heads."

Jack chuckled, "I've attended a lot of lectures over the years, and that's one thing she never did. She was as down to earth as she could be."

Kendra smiled at the idea. "Sometimes, but other times she was the picture of an absent minded professor. I remember going to a pub once with Aunt Mary and some friends, and she struggled to open a bag of chips.

Jack laughed. He could picture it well.

"She was quite taken with you, did you know that?"

"Really? I had no idea. That's nice to hear."

"She always thought you'd missed your calling."

"And be a priest? No thank you. I'm quite happy doing what I'm doing."

"Professor, actually. She didn't understand why you went into law enforcement when you could have taught Religious Studies. She was always impressed by the way you could break down complicated ideas so even a beginner could understand," Kendra said earnestly. "She'd be happy to know you solve hate crimes now."

Jack said nothing, he just smiled and held his hand out to Kendra. She took it and together they left the office.

THEY ARRIVED AT *Bet-Neshar* twenty minutes later, and surveyed the scene. Their first visit had been rushed, but in the quiet of early evening it looked like a whole different place. "Aside from the murder, this is really a beautiful place," Kendra started.

"Yeah... I see that the memorial is working its way up the stairs." Jack pointed towards the front of the house.

"Hmmm," Kendra crossed her arms and tilted her head to study him. "I know that look."

"Interesting. Anthropological theory says these roadside memorials are a result of our culture not having a common voice to express its grief. Statistics show a direct connection between decreasing involvement in church with an increase in this type of impromptu display."

"So..."

"Isn't it strange that a place full of religious people would be making such a secular display?" Jack concluded.

"Mmmm, you've got a point, and it also speaks to this place not really being much more than a religious flop-house."

"Intentional community, if you wouldn't mind," said a voice from behind them.

Kendra and Jack turned in surprise to see a woman in her 30's, briefcase in hand, looking as if the strain of the day had already gotten the better of her.

Quickly noticing the badge Jack wore, the woman held out her hand to shake Jack's hand first. "Amanda Morgan," she said. "I helped Joan run this place. I was the business person behind her vision."

"Kendra Ward and Jack Hudson," replied Jack, shaking Amanda's hand. "Were you and *Tricia* close?"

"Ah," she smiled," you've found our little secret, and I expect you have questions. Do you mind if we speak inside? I'd like to be out of these shoes and away from the curious."

"By all means," Kendra said, gesturing for Amanda to take lead.

The three walked out to the road away from the crime scene, and up to another building. "This really is a beautiful setting. I didn't get a chance to look around when I was here earlier, and I didn't realize this place was so big."

"Yes it is. Most of the houses date back almost a century or more, which is quite something even around here. Tricia loved it," Amanda replied.

She led them up the hill towards another older house Inside was an office that looked out of place in a religious community. "This one is mine," she said. Kendra and Jack quickly looked around looking at the sleek decor. Sitting behind the desk she gestured towards the guest chairs. "Before we begin, can you please tell me something? Was it quick?"

"Was what quick?" Jack asked.

"Tricia's death. I don't know the details. Please tell me she wasn't in pain."

"I can promise you that," Kendra nodded reassuringly. "Tricia would not have known what was happening. I am curious though, when did you get word of her death? Don't you live here?"

"Mmm... around seven yesterday morning, and no I don't live here. I'm based in Halifax. I drove up here as soon as I could. I had a phone call saying the police were at the chapel and that Joan... well, Tricia, was dead."

"Based?" Jack asked.

Amanda shrugged, "It's where the money is. It's where Tricia and I grew up. It's home. I fundraise and deal with all the money and legalities down there, and Tricia was free to be up here without worrying about anything."

Seeing the look on Jack's face, Amanda continued, "It worked for us. Look, we're a registered non-profit, and I have the books looked at regularly to show everything is done according to the law. This worked for both Tricia and myself. She always had a vision of doing something like this in a small town, and I was able to do work that really mattered while remaining at home. It was good.

"Who called?"

"Sister Margaret. She was given special dispensation to speak during Holy Week, so she had to call me."

"No one else would have called you?" Jack asked.

"No, nobody here would do that. Everyone was under a vow of silence for Holy Week."

Kendra seemed surprised, "That's not a normal requirement."

"No it's not, but these aren't average people. We have some pilgrims from other countries who don't speak English, we've got some people who were living on the street with nowhere else to go, we've got some people who would rather live in community than in their own home, we've got former nuns and priests. It's a real mix of people, and the one thing they could all equally give this week was their voice."

Kendra nodded her understanding. "My people said they didn't get far when they were questioning witnesses. Have there been agreements signed? Do you have a list of the people who live here?"

"Some of them, the more socially conscious, but because we don't turn anyone away, we might have them show up for dinner and be gone from their room by the next morning. They don't have to give us a name: that was Tricia's vision. She believed God knew who they were, so why should we make it an issue."

Kendra and Jack looked at each other, realizing that just threw the pool of suspects wide open again.

"Look," Amanda continued, having watched their reactions, "I'm sure in your world of regulation and files and deadlines, this seems completely illogical, and believe me when I tell you I often have to do back-flips for banks and legislators on this matter. But the truth of it is most people who come here are already off the grid. Immigrants who don't even know their birthdate, alcoholics who can't remember their last name, prostitutes who want to be anybody else, couples trying to escape society's expectations."

"And the children?"

"That is the exception. We don't have any children here at the moment, but when we have children they are properly documented. We don't want to go completely against the law and be shut down. We just want this place to be a true sanctuary."

"Do you have any kind of list about visitors or residents?" Jack asked.

"We have room assignments. I can print those for you. We don't keep paperwork at the office. Everything we have is on my computer and Tricia's."

"We already have Tricia's computer," Jack informed her. "But if you don't mind me asking, why is she called Pope Joan?"

Amanda smiled, "She's been called that since High School. Even back then she challenged the priest where we grew up. She was one of the first to be an altar-girl. She never gave up her dream of being able to officiate at the sacraments, but if they weren't going to let her in the front door, she'd come in the side, she always said. She wanted to be like Pope Joan: spent most of her time studying and serve others. Being a woman might have added to the challenge, but it didn't take away from the goal."

"Pope Joan had some other characteristics," Kendra continued, "and historians agreed she wouldn't have gotten very far without her lovers. Did Tricia Steward have the same advantages?"

"No one here expected a vow of chastity, if that's what you're asking. She wasn't a virgin, but she wasn't a whore either. Look, things have to change sometime. Women are half of the population but we still aren't allowed to just be ourselves. Tricia had books given to her by her favourite professor that proved women had these roles in the early church, but as things became more structured and when there was more money to gain, men started pushing women out, calling them demons, removing them from history. Tricia chose the name 'Pope Joan' to share the truth with others. She had every right to be here and to do what she was doing. Just because the church wasn't ready for her didn't mean that God wasn't."

"We're not here to judge Tricia's choices," Kendra tried to reassure Amanda, "we're here to find her killer."

Amanda tented her hands and leaned forward, "Sorry... sorry... old defenses die hard. Both Tricia and I have had our share of justifying our sexual choices in a world where people assume things about religious types."

"With whom?"

"Professors, old priests, family members, neighbours... every once in awhile we'd find someone who was also convinced that the church wouldn't have as many sex scandals if it didn't take such a hard line on celibacy, but mostly people just assume women interested in the church are there because they can't function as sexually mature adults."

"Anyone recently challenge Tricia that way? Someone from her past, perhaps someone who went to school with her."

Amanda looked off in the distance, trying to think of anyone who would fit that bill."

"No...no, I can't think of anyone. I know she was enjoying a visit from an old school friend who came to stay about a month ago, but I don't recall him insulting her."

Pulling his interview notepad and pen from his jacket pocket, Jack nodded, "Do you have a name? Perhaps a room number and a description?"

"Ah... Jim Davis, Father James Davis, I believe. After he was ordained he went to India. He lived there for about ten years, then came home and has been looking for a place to work."

"Catholic?"

"No, Anglican. He grew up in England, emigrated here when he was a teenager."

"That's a tough age to move anywhere," Jack said. "And what was his attitude towards women priests?"

"Completely against. Not even a hint that he could be otherwise convinced. Jesus was male, so therefore all priests had to be male. They even had a debate about it in the main building the other night. Everyone was there. We opened the doors to the chapel and library, and people were sitting in the dining room. It got crowded. Jim said his bit about Jesus being male, and Tricia countered by saying Jesus had to be a man in that culture to be listened to. But he didn't have any other power in that society like wealth or family status. She argued that the second coming would be a woman, probably handicapped and poor."

"Just like the people who live here."

"Just like the people who live everywhere and get forgotten."

Nodding, Kendra looked at Jack who returned to his line of questioning. "Can you give us a description of Fr. Davis?"

"Early 40's, tall, athletic, light blonde hair, really pale skin, always wore black, glasses, blue eyes, I think. He spent a lot of time in the library. He told Tricia a few times that the books she had in the library were biased and that she should have some really solid theological books in there so the people who live here would have a better understanding of how the church really worked. Tricia didn't agree with him, needless to say."

"Better understanding of the church? What was he recommending?"

"He threw a lot of titles around but I didn't catch them. Tricia was the theologian. I'm just the business person. But from what she told me, it was a lot of stuff that argued Jesus being male was the most important thing, and about how it was historical fact that men spread the Christian faith through the world. Tricia told him he was full of it, that wives and mothers had more influence on the many generations of the church than a priest ever did."

"Well, I agree with her on that point," Kendra said. "You were witness to all of this?"

"This past week? Yeah, I saw it. I've never come so close to wanting to hurt a priest before in my life as this guy. He was arrogant as anything. But Tricia would just laugh at him and throw her arms around his neck in a big hug. She'd say she was happy he never changed, and that she would be the one who would ultimately change his mind. Nothing he said ever got to Tricia. I'd walk away, but she'd just shrug it off."

"How did she manage that?"

"I don't know. She'd just say when you have the truth on your side, you didn't have to work that hard to make it happen. Tricia would just say she knew he was wrong, and one day everyone would understand that he was wrong. She said you could never convince anyone through words, you had to do it through actions. She really believed if people spend time in community with the outcasts of the world, they would really find God there and realize the hierarchy of the church is morally bankrupt. She said Jesus had no time for the people in charge, so she didn't either. She said she might disagree completely with Jim's attitude towards women, but deep down he was one of the good guys and he deserved her support as much as the next person."

"Sounds rather altruistic and naive," Jack muttered.

"Yeah, it was..." Amanda said wistfully. "But she really believed it, and she lived it as much as she could."

"So you couldn't stand Fr. Davis. Was he the reason you went back to the city?"

"Perhaps a little, I really didn't want to be around him. But it was Easter, and I wanted to be with my family."

"And what room was his?"

"Top floor in the large building across the street, last door on your right."

Jack flipped his book shut and looked at Kendra. "The Upper Room," he said.

CHAPTER EIGHT

"HUGH," KENDRA SPOKE into her phone, "where is everyone now?"

She and Jack had left Amanda in the office, and had climbed the stairs to Fr. Davis' room. The door was unlocked, which didn't necessarily mean anything in a place like this, but it was certainly worth noting. Inside they found the room neat and orderly. There was a bible on the beside table, a suit in the closet, with the rest of his clothing folded neatly in the drawers. On top of the dresser there was a small, square box with a crucifix carved into the top. Jack pointed at it while Kendra was on the phone. When she nodded, he opened it to find a small chalice and paten, two glass cruets and a box for the host. Folded into a pocket in the top were a prayer stole and some Eucharistic linens.

"Seems to be all there," Kendra said, putting her phone in her pocket. "Hugh is just outside in the parking lot by the last residential building down the street."

Jack walked over to the window and saw it faced a thin strip of trees before opening onto the Baie de Chaleur. "Quite the view from up here. If you look, you can see the graveyard goes back to the tree line. There should be a fence a little further back separating the graveyard's property from a green space owned by the old mill."

"Green space?" Kendra joined Jack at the window. "That means no one was close enough to see anything."

"Yup," he sighed, looking around the room once more. "I can't see anything else here, Kendra. It hardly looks like anyone has been here let alone committed murder here."

"That's true. On the way out we'll tape up the door anyway. If Fr. Davis returns, that will force him to come find us, and in the meantime it will keep others out. We still might find something here."

"I'll send Eli up to do another search when we get downstairs. We should check in with Hugh to see who's done what."

Kendra nodded and they left the room, stopping only long enough for Jack to put a large taped 'X' over the doorway.

They found Hugh beside his rental car, a huge map spread across the hood.

"What have we got?" Kendra asked as she joined him.

"Everyone else is going door to door in both these buildings, checking the residents. Unfortunately, word got out that we were here and some have decided to vacate the premises. Since we're getting the silent treatment, we're not getting too far. I imagine getting prints in here is like picking up confetti, so I doubt that's going to be helpful. We don't have anything to compare them to anyway."

"It's a small town," Kendra stated, "people can't go too far."

Jack cleared his throat, "Ah, have you taken a good look around?" Pointing as he turned in a circle he said, "Just beyond all these trees is an international seaport, deep enough for some pretty big cruise ships I've been told. We've got bus and train lines and at least three highways out of town. And that's before you consider the private airport and personal boats. This place might be small, but there are a lot of ways in and out."

Sighing, Kendra nodded in understanding. "Perfect location for a community that welcomes tourists and prodigals in equal measure. Do we have a timeline up yet?"

"Posted? No. But Eli is keeping one on that computer of his," Hugh replied.

"Good," Jack said as he kept looking past the graveyard towards the tree line. "We might want to consider a parallel timeline with Holy Week. I don't know if the extra timeline is going to mean anything, but it's good to keep following. We had the welcoming of guests like Palm Sunday, then a debate that was like a cleansing of the temple between Tricia and her friend Davis. Tricia was raped, mutilated, murdered, the nails removed, and placed on the altar before the body was discovered, which means we were already through most of the Good Friday story before we even started." Jack turned to Kendra as he spoke, "What else happened that might help us?"

"The tomb we've got. But we still don't know who her killer was, so he could be her Pilate or her Roman soldier. There's no way to know."

Hugh's head snapped up, "What are you saying now?"

"Pilate was the Roman official who ordered Jesus' death while the Roman soldier realized they had killed the Messiah and he fell to the ground when he realized the truth," Kendra replied.

Nodding in understanding, Hugh spoke to Kendra again, "So are you thinking we might be looking for someone who felt they could judge Tricia, or someone who feels guilty when they realized what they'd done?"

"I'm not sure, but when Theresa said this killer couldn't decide if he loved her or hated her, it got me thinking. We might be dealing with someone who is battling their own demons."

"Or mental illness."

"Exactly. Most times they are the same thing. So what do you think we have to do next?" Kendra asked, looking from Jack to Hugh.

"Damned if I know, Kenny," Hugh said in exasperation. "The motive on this one can go any number of ways, but we've got almost nothing for physical evidence, and the number of people with opportunity is endless. It seems the more we try to fill in the blanks, the more questions we find. We were able to confirm earlier that she was the priest at worship Thursday night, and then everyone left to go back to their rooms. So we've got a window between 11:00 PM and 4:00 AM local, when the murder was called in." Scratching his head, Hugh moved around his car. "Outside of that we've got nothing. Where was she raped and mutilated? How did the killer get her body into the chapel with no one seeing? How did he clean up the evidence?"

"I think we can answer one of those," Yasmin came up behind them accompanied by an elderly woman.

"I'm Sister Margaret," the woman announced, "but right now I'm feeling more like Magdalene, and not having her luck." The older woman wheezed a chuckle as all eyes turned to her.

Hugh leaned over the Jack and whispered, "What she mean by that?"

“Mary Magdalene watched Jesus die and was the first to find him alive on Easter morning, then went to tell everyone,” Jack whispered back.

“But the victim is dead, not alive. I don’t get the joke.”

Jack shrugged, “Yeah well, Mary Magdalene was the first to announce Jesus was alive, so the church recognizes her as the first Apostle. Lots see that as the reason women should be leaders too.”

“But she was a prostitute.”

“Nope, the only thing we know about Magdalene is she has seven demons and was the only witness to Jesus’ death and resurrection in all four gospels. The prostitute stuff came centuries later.”

Hugh looked puzzled by what Jack told him, but they both turned back to Sister Margaret to hear what she had to say.

“After I found Joan yesterday morning I called the police and Amanda, then I went for a walk to pray for strength and guidance. I found a small fire pit that had been recently used, as well as pillows and two used condoms.”

“Well,” Hugh huffed grimly, “looks like we’re getting somewhere at last.” Then he turned to Sister Margaret, “And did you just say you left the scene of a murder?”

“Why are you just telling us now?” Kendra asked, crossing her arms in authority.

“Well I’m here, aren’t I!” the nun replied angrily. “I did my duty. I called in the crime scene without disturbing anything. I called Amanda so she could do what she needed to do, and now I’m here telling you what I found. What more do you want me to do?”

Kendra closed her eyes and shook her head. "I'm sorry," she said when she looked at the elderly woman again. "Yes, you have been a great help. Can you show us where you found the fire and other things?"

"Of course. That's why I spoke to this lovely young woman," Sister Margaret said taking Yasmin by the hand and pulling her towards the graveyard.

Hugh put the map in the car quickly then caught up with the group as they walked up the street, through the graveyard and into the woods. They were all grateful that Easter was so late in the spring and that winter had been easy, so there wasn't much snow.

The site they saw was far enough in the trees that anyone from the street or the neighbouring buildings would never have seen anyone was in there. A little way into the woods they found a small area, less then ten meters square, with the telltale signs of a fire off to one side.

"Look at this, Kendra," Yasmin pointed at two pillows with burned holes in the middle where spikes could have been. "And there's rope scattered here and there."

Kendra nodded. "Take pictures the best way you can. It's too dark to see much with all these trees, but the flash and our head lamps should show most of it. Whoever did this chose the spot well. Even that fire wouldn't have produced enough smoke to be seen."

"Maybe, but the path is well worn," Jack countered. "This place isn't a secret, either. Look how the brush is cut back far enough so anyone could have carried a body in and out of here easily. The last of the snow is packed pretty tight."

"You're right. But we still have to work with the presumption it was fairly private, because surely a woman having spikes driving into her hands and ankles would have been reported by a witness."

"You thinking no one would care about the rape, Kendra?" Yasmin asked. She was the member of the team most experienced in sexual harassment and abuse.

"Unfortunately, if she was drugged, she wouldn't have put up a struggle or it might not have looked like rape. We'll gather what we can after the pictures, I don't want to take the chance that we've overlooked anything helpful. Everything will need to be analyzed so be careful."

"And what do you think the cloth is, Kendra?" Hugh asked, looking at the ground. "That's a whole lot of torn black fabric where the victim was tied with rope."

"If I had to guess," Theresa offered, "that looks like rent garments."

Hugh looked confused, "Rent?".

Kendra squatted down beside some of the fabric, "In church language 'to rend a garment' means to tear your clothing with a lot of force. It's usually associated with extreme grief. It's very melodramatic. Maybe our suspect was dealing with a lot of guilt."

"As he should be," Sister Margaret pronounced.

"Kendra," Jack called, having gone down another path while everyone was talking. "I think you want to see this."

Kendra led the others towards Jack, and stopped when she saw what he had discovered. "Damn it!"

CHAPTER NINE

Judas, being one of the twelve closest to Jesus, began to question what was happening. Was the Lord truly taking them to the Holy City and certain death? As the days passed one to another, he became more uncomfortable with what was happening and knew Jesus had to be stopped. Stealing away one evening, he found the Temple Priests and told them he would deliver Jesus to them. The Sanhedrin thanked him and gave him thirty pieces of Silver.

"I don't want this," Judas told them

"Take it, do good for others if you don't want it yourself."

So Judas took the money and waited for an opportunity. Not many days later, at the first evening of the Feast of the Passover, Judas and many of the others were sitting in the Upper Room with Jesus. Again Jesus was talking about many thing, both understandable and cryptic. Judas hadn't really been paying attention until he heard the word "betray". Quickly he raised his head and challenged Jesus. They spoke roughly to each other and finally Jesus said "Do as you have to do."

Judas was so angry and hurt, he got up from the table and left the room. The silver coins were heavy in his purse, but no heavier then his heart, as he stormed toward the Temple.

"You really want him?" he practically screamed at the priests, "you can have him. Come with me."

Swiftly they walked through the streets, across the bridge and out the gates of the city, until they got to the Garden of Gethsemane. Jesus had been praying by himself, and looked up when Judas approached. When Judas kissed him on the cheek, Jesus did not move, but rather looked at one of his favoured followers and asked "By a kiss, Judas?"

The soldiers led Jesus away in ropes, and the other disciples scattered. Only Judas remained in the garden to watch and realize what had happened. How did his anger get him to this point?

The next day was full of gossip, news and finally death. Judas was overcome with guilt and grief. "Why did you kill him?" he demanded of the Sanhedrin. "I thought you would only arrest him, jail him and let him come to his senses. I didn't agree to killing him."

"Be quiet," the High Priest snapped, "you did your duty to God, you've been well paid. What did you think was going to happen?"

"I didn't agree to this," Judas cried again.

"That's your problem," the High Priest responded, then laughed at Judas when he threw the money from his purse on the ground and ran away.

Not many hours later, the body of Judas was found hanging in a tree, not far from where he betrayed the one he loved.

A story from The Gospel of Christ

Praise to you, Lord Jesus Christ

THE GROUND UNDERNEATH was littered with eye glasses, more black cloth, pictures of Tricia in happier times and a narrow, white plastic tab that had once been the distinguishing feature in a priests' shirt.

"Son of a bitch," Hugh said from behind having followed Jack and Kendra down the path.

Kendra shook her head and crossed her arms. She hated when things went in this direction.

"Explains why we didn't have any evidence of Fr. Davis being in his room recently," Jack commented, as he looked at the body hanging from the tree, swinging slightly under its own weight. Around his neck was a sign that read "Iudas".

"This is one part of the story I really could have done without," Kendra said to no one in particular.

Yasmin and Sister Margaret had followed Jack and Kendra down the path. Coming closer Sister Margaret crossed herself, "He deserved a different kind of justice."

"We can't totally rule out foul play, Kenny, given the circumstances."

Putting a comforting arm around the Sister, Kendra shook her head, "No Hugh, we can't. But I'm thinking the odds of that are slim to none. Call the RCMP. They aren't going to be happy with another body."

"Look at these," Yasmin started, holding some of the pictures in her hand. "I guess I was right after all. He did love her and hate her."

Kendra looked over at the pictures Yasmin held in her hands, and reached for them. She saw that Tricia and Jim Davis smiled back at her in one, laughed about a private joke in another, and bowed their heads together in a third. "Look at this one," Kendra pointed back at Theresa, showing her a picture of a smiling Tricia with a less-than-pleased looking Jim in the background.

"There's history there. I'm going to go see what I can find."

Kendra called out as Yasmin left with Sister Margaret, "Find Eli and tell him to update the timeline with what we've found."

"I'm going to call the RCMP and take a bit of a breather," Hugh called as he left the opening.

Kendra and Jack were left alone, looking at the new body. "What are you thinking?" Jack asked her.

"Mmm... just how much passion there was between these two and how it was never properly realized. How their calls to ministry were so similar and yet so different. How she trusted him with her mind but not her heart, and he wanted it all. Did he rape her because she said no or because she said yes? Was he drugged too, or just her? How long had he been thinking about doing this, because it obviously wasn't a last minute decision. This was calculated. Look at the wording around his neck, it isn't even in English. What made him do this? Any of it?"

"These methodical types usually leave a diary or journal somewhere so those of us cleaning up the mess can understand their motives."

"I wonder where he left it. It wasn't in his room."

"I dunno, we didn't touch the Bible on his bedside table. That would be my first guess."

"Mmm, true," she nodded. "Look at the noose. I think that's the same rope that he used to tie Tricia to the pillows. It looks crude enough."

"That would make sense. It tied them both to their fate. There's symmetry in that."

"Yes, and if there's one thing we know for sure in this murder, it's deeply symbolic. I know Hugh is right, that all murders make a statement, but this one... this one..." Kendra shook her head, lost for words.

"Hey," Jack said, moving behind her and squeezing her shoulders, "we can be pretty sure we don't have a psycho on the loose, that's good news."

Kendra chuckled, "Sometimes what stands for 'good news' in this job really makes me wonder."

Jack chuckled with her, then they both grew sober again. Tilting his head to the side, Jack pulled gloves from his back pocket and approached Fr. Davis' body. Lifting his left hand, Jack looked at it more closely, then glanced over at Kendra.

"What did you find?" she asked, coming closer herself.

"Third degree burn blisters on his left hand, meaning he probably held the spikes with his bare hands as he pounded them into her. We'll need the lab to confirm, but if he has blisters then there was some real time between when he mutilated her and when he died."

"It is possible that someone hung him up here in retaliation for her death."

"True, but I think we would have seen more signs of a struggle."

"His clothes get torn while he fights someone, his glasses are pulled off, they get the jump on him and hoist him, and then put the sign around his neck. He obviously loved Tricia, so maybe..." Kendra trailed off.

"Maybe," Jack continued, "but if this was their Garden of Gethsemane...."

"...then there wouldn't have been others here," Kendra nodded as she finished the sentence.

"Right, there's no way I can figure this, that he brought her out here after Maundy Thursday Mass, drugged her, tied her, raped her, banged spikes in her hands and ankles, pulled them out and washed her, snuck back into the chapel with her body, prepared the table, then came back out here and killed himself. That's a whole lot of activity for one man in a three-to-four hour window. And with two used condoms? The sex alone at his age and I assume inexperience, would have taken close to an hour. He still had to tie her feet together before shoving the spike in."

"I guess we won't really know until you get something back from the lab. We also need to compare the paper and handwriting around his neck, with the verse shoved in Tricia's mouth." Kendra nodded. "Oh, Jack," she breathed deeply, "I'll be so glad when this evidence starts giving us answers rather than just more questions."

"You and me both, Pal, you and me both...."

CHAPTER TEN

LATER THAT EVENING they gathered back at the RCMP detachment. "It's going to be a while before the lab comes back with anything, Kendra, maybe not until next week," Eli said as he came up behind Kendra, who was stared out the window into the dark.

"I know," she sighed.

Eli was about to move on when Kendra started. "I just can't help thinking that a couple of days ago Tricia Steward was preparing to preside at Maundy Thursday service. She was probably fulfilling a promise to herself because the church wasn't going to do it. Maybe she had been working on her sermon for weeks... months.... years... Did she vest or was she dressed casually? Did she have any acolytes or assistants? Did she prepare to wash the feet of the man who would ultimately kill her? Did she spend the day in prayer or in busywork? Did she plan ahead to her Good Friday service or was she a one-ceremony-at-a-time presider. Did she have an Easter Vigil in her Holy Week plans? Was she going to watch the sun come up Easter morning? Did she look forward to this time every year or did the season surprise her by how quickly it came after Christmas? Did she fast and pray the entire forty days, or was this the only week that she put effort into?"

"I found an online journal that she kept. It might help you feel more connected if you read it. I can set it up on your computer."

Kendra smiled at Eli, "Sorry... I was getting whimsical when this case needs clear thinking."

"I don't know about that. I think when we get lulls during an investigation, we all start to wonder about the victims and the killers. I think it comes pretty naturally to all of us to relate to the victim. Doesn't mean we aren't clear minded and professional when it's needed, it just means they matter to us."

"Thank you for that, Eli, and get me her diary."

Eli nodded and picked up his computer, while Kendra remained at the window for a few moments then sat down on the edge of the desk.

"Where are we now?" Kendra asked her team.

Theresa looked up at her and leaned back into her chair. "Well, there is definitely a long history between Tricia and Fr. Davis. They met in grad school and shared many of the same classes. Apparently he took courses with your aunt as well, but after some arguments he dropped the class. He didn't like what Dr. Schuller was teaching."

"Can't say that surprises me," Kendra commented offhandedly. "Go on..."

"Right. Well like Eli said lab work will have to wait because of the holidays. Jack grabbed the things from Davis' room..."

"Yeah, the room..." Jack started, "looks like Davis did leave a few notes on a folded sheet in his Bible, but so far it's not explaining too much."

"So you think there is a second journal somewhere, or is this just a killer who doesn't fit the profile?"

"Well... I'm starting to think he took it all to confession rather than writing it for anyone else to see."

"Confession need a priest," Theresa offered hopefully.

"Not in the English Church."

"The what?" Yasmin asked

Jack looked over his shoulder at her and said, "It's just shorthand, Yasmin. Calling something the Roman church means Roman Catholic, Russian means Russian Orthodox, English means Anglican or Episcopalians, German is Lutherans. It's not a perfect system, but it usually works."

Kendra saw Theresa close her mouth shake her head, and couldn't help smiling to herself. If nothing else, her team was getting an education on church traditions.

"Okay, I'll bite. Why don't priests in the 'English' church hear confessions?" Eli asked the obvious question.

"It's all in the theology. Those in the Roman Catholic and Orthodox churches believe the priests are their first connection to God, but the Reformed and Protestants feel we can speak to God directly, without anyone else getting involved. Sometimes we have priests for confessions, but it's not common." Kendra answered him.

Jack nodded, "Yeah, they call themselves Anglo-Catholics, high church and traditional, when they confess to priests. But regular churches have personal confession. If this Fr. Davis could find an Anglo-Catholic parish, he might have confessed to that priest. Otherwise I don't think he left us anything to go on."

"Okay, I agree it's a long shot, but it's one worth taking. Jack, could you?"

Nodding Jack pulled out his phone.

"Good, okay Theresa, what else?"

"Not much until reports come back. Otherwise we've just been going through Tricia's computer to see what we can find. Thankfully she was very comfortable with technology, and kept everything on her computer from personal emails to business for *Bet-Neshar* and her personal journal. We're just seeing if any of that is helpful."

"Yeah Kendra," Eli interrupted, "I set up the link to her journal pages on your computer. I sent it to Jack too."

"Link?" Kendra was surprised he hadn't just emailed them to her.

"They're extensive, Kendra," Theresa interrupted, "and I don't understand a whole lot of what she was talking about. It seems like she's almost... praying, if that makes sense?"

"A prayer journal," Kendra nodded, "yes, that does make sense. I'll read it and see if I find anything important. Alright everyone, this sounds good. We can't do anything now so head over to the hotel. We've been at this for two days straight, and I'm exhausted so you must be dead on our feet."

"No pun intended," Hugh said under his breath, bringing a chuckle to the room.

IN HER HOTEL ROOM KENDRA made a cup of tea then offered up a small prayer of her own that they would soon have a clearer picture of the entire situation. By the time she sat down to her computer, she felt better prepared to see what Tricia had been writing.

Lord, I confess that I've sinned against you in thought, word and deed, by those things I have done and those things which I ought to have done.... and I didn't. I'm so sorry I didn't take care of those children today. It broke my heart to let them leave, but I know their mother is a good person. I wish I could help her, but it has to be her choice. Please forgive me for not being stronger and insisting that family stay. And please bring them back so we will have another chance to make a difference in their lives.

I lift mine eyes, mine eyes to the mountains. Today was so beautiful. Thank you, gracious Creator. Seeing those paths being cleared through the trees and being able to walk up behind our community was such a blessing. The old mill has agreed to remove the fencing along the new pathways, and plant some new shrubs to better mark the entrances. Thank you so much for opening their minds. It will be a great addition to our landscape, and the people in this town will also get the benefit of walking along the new paths. Perhaps someday we will be able to make the docks so attractive that every kind of cruise ship will pull into the harbour. I hope so, anyway.

I filmed this video today while I was walking. What a funny animal. I don't think the squirrel knew he had an audience. Amanda will probably give me hell for not finishing the statements, but this was worth it.

MAKING A NOTE TO ASK Eli if they had videos or found a camera anywhere, Kendra continued.

Song of Songs and dear old Solomon had it right... tonight's Saturday night special is the way to go. Chapter five, verse one and counting...I do love being the honeycomb!

Kendra was so surprised she had to laugh and could only assume Tricia had been talking about the Song of Songs in the Bible. Amanda had said neither she nor Tricia were celibate, and that seemed about right. Kendra quickly scrolled through the Song of Solomon on her phone, and smiled when she reached the relevant passage. "I'm so glad you had this in your life," she whispered to Tricia's memory.

The phone rang and startled her.

"Hey Kenny, someone likes us," the tired voice of Jack began. "I guess the lab was bored. Anyway we got a preliminary."

"Already?"

"Yup. Same rope, only sign of one user so our theory of a struggle with a third party is pretty well nixed. They're calling it suicide. Fibers under his nails include the rope, his torn robe and cells from Tricia's body. The burns were pretty bad on his left hand and would have hurt like a bugger. How he held those spikes and drove them in is beyond me. Fluids from the vic were on his hands, groin and in his mouth, so he's our rapist. His right hand is bruised from using a stone or brick, which explains why we didn't find a mallet or big hammer. And his right hand has an ink stain that matches both the sign around his neck and the note in Tricia's mouth."

"Okay.... I guess that wraps it up."

"Not quite. Time of Davis' death is estimated to be roughly two hours before Tricia's."

"Before?" Kendra's head snapped up.

"That's what it says. And no oil or soap like we found on Tricia's body."

"So we have another killer?"

"Nope, we don't have her killer. We have the guy who raped and mutilated her, but someone else ended her life."

"Oh my God...."

"You got that right, and here's what I'm thinking, even drugged she would have felt pain but might not have been aware what was going on. That could make her pass out and look dead. There were stones everywhere and the rope had dirt in it, so it wasn't new. Maybe this wasn't planned like we thought. Oh, and they found drugs in his pocket. Rohypnol."

Kendra rubbed her temples, "I've been reading her journal, and she talks about removing a fence behind the tree line that divided the graveyard from the paths on the old mill's property. She also talked about them planting shrubs to make sure everyone could see the proper entry and exist points to the path. Do you think Fr. Davis used a stone because he couldn't find a hammer lying around, but the other items, the spikes and previously cut rope, were leftovers from the fence they removed and the shrubs planted? Perhaps the project that hadn't been cleaned properly before winter? The torn clothing, glasses and used condoms were definitely his, but they were all something he came into the woods with anyway. Do you think he just grabbed the spikes and rope from the litter around him? The fire would have burned off a lot of the extra residue"

"But what about the pillows?" Jack asked.

"Maybe he was setting up a love nest against the snow. Maybe he had hoped she would join him willingly."

"Still doesn't explain why Davis got the spikes hot," Jack pointed out.

"No it doesn't," she agreed, "but we already know there was a small fire there. Maybe the spikes removed from the fence were inside the pit already, or maybe in his haste he kicked them in. Or maybe, as we originally suspected, he purposely put the spikes in the fire to nail her. None of that really matters now, but if there are other spikes in the area, this might be as a crime of passion rather than pre-meditated."

"And the rape?"

"Oh, rape is rape, there's no excuse for that one. Fr. Davis was a rapist, and I will file that truth with anyone who asks and many who won't. But somewhere along the way, his misplaced sense of affection for Tricia changed into hatred and blind rage. Did that happen in the clearing or before? That's the difference."

"Let's run this down," Jack continued. "He brought Tricia into the clearing in the woods after Maundy Thursday service, which we don't know if he even attended. He drugs her either before or after. He rapes her, which was definitely pre-meditated because of the pills and condoms. He ties her to the pillows with rope he either cut and brought with him or found lying around. He nails her hands into the pillow with spikes either consciously or unconsciously heated in the fire he set. He burns his hands in the process, but his pain seems nothing to him. He watches her twist in agony and then probably rapes her again, using yet another condom. Why this level of self-protection, I don't know. Then he ties her feet, nails her ankles with another spike, watches her pass out. He gets up, believing he's killed her. His rage is replaced with grief. He walks around a bit tearing his clothing, then walks off to a tree either taking more rope with him or finding that lying around too. He makes a noose, writes a sign and puts it around his neck, climbs the tree to tie the rope, then falls with it around his neck, basically killing himself as he gazes in the direction of the woman he loves, who he thinks he already killed."

"Sounds plausible."

"That would also explain why he didn't leave any confession behind," Jack added. "It's as good a working theory as any."

"Yes, but it's still not our killing moment, so what is?"

"That would be the sword into the side. It sliced her liver, cut through her lung and nicked her heart, which made her bled out. That was the real cause of death."

"So, whomever placed her on that table and prepared it for Eucharist, was the actual killer. I wonder if she regained consciousness."

"That's hard to say. If the spike in her ankles caused her to pass out, then any movement would have continued the pain and kept her unconscious. Removing the spikes would have been excruciating. It's quite possible that the person who found her thought she was already dead..."

"And they wouldn't know they were the actual murderer," Kendra finished the thought.

"Who could do that?" Jack wondered.

"Someone strong enough to carry her and pull out the spikes. Someone who knew how to set the table for Mass and prepare a dead body. Someone who thought she was the ultimate sacrifice. Mental illness or strong devotion?" Kendra asked into the phone.

"Both, maybe."

CHAPTER ELEVEN

THE NEXT MORNING WAS Sunday, so Kendra and her team joined those from the town as they gathered around the old light house. It was still dark and the snow made it feel even colder than the normal early morning temperature. During their investigation Eli discovered this was an annual Easter Sunday tradition in Dalhousie. Locals from the different churches gathered to sing, listen to the Easter story and pray, as they watch the morning sun rise over the water. "Christ has Risen!" one of the leaders shouted.

"He is risen indeed!" came the response all around them.

Kendra and Jack added their voices to the response, but the rest stood around not knowing what to do.

"You coming for breakfast?" a little girl about ten years old asked.

"Breakfast?" Yasmin asked.

"Yeah, we go to breakfast after this. It's not at my church this year, it's at the other one. I hope they have pancakes this time. I miss pancakes."

Yasmin looked at Kendra and mouthed "pancakes" with a questioning look on her face.

"I'll explain later." Kendra said then smiled at the little girl, "I think we will just have breakfast by ourselves this morning, but thank you. Enjoy your breakfast and I hope you have pancakes."

"Me too!" the little girl smiled, then turned to run after the group.

"So you going to tell me what that was about?" Yasmin asked after everyone from the town left. Jack was still staring out over the water, but Huge, Eli and Theresa had left.

"I imagine her family does a fast during Lent. They have pancakes on Shrove Tuesday, the day before Lent starts, then they don't eat sugar or oil until Easter morning." Anticipating the next question, Kendra continued, "Most people don't do that, or if they fast it's usually things like giving up chocolate or coffee. I guess her family is more religious, and given that she's now holding that priest's hand, I bet she's the priest's daughter."

"My Grandmother was Baptist," Yasmin said quietly.

"Oh?"

"Yeah, I went to church with her once or twice when I was a kid. I just remember it being really hot and really long. The music was good, though."

Kendra smiled, "Yes, I bet it was. I never grew up with gospel music around me, but I go to concerts every chance I get. There have been some really good composers over the years."

"I don't really get this..."

"Which part?"

"Any of it. I don't understand what all the symbols mean and the bowing.... I've never seen that."

"No, you wouldn't have."

"Why is that? Because it was Baptist? Jack said something about Catholics being opposite Protestants, but that doesn't mean anything to me."

Kendra smiled, "Not opposite, exactly. Just different. The Roman Church has been around since the beginning of Christianity, almost 2000 years. But about seven or eight hundred years ago, a group of people started protesting over all the rules and restrictions of the Church. Thousands were killed for wanting the church to change. The first ones to make it stick are who we call the Reformers around 1500 CE. Martin Luther, John Calvin, Thomas Cranmer, men like that. Those who followed them considered themselves part of the Reformation, like our victim Tricia, and her rapist. After that, others came along who thought the reforms didn't go far enough. Men like John Wesley, um... George Fox... John Knox. They didn't like how the Reformers still did a lot of things the way the Catholics did, so they got rid of the bowing and weekly Eucharist, they destroyed art and music. It was a really sad time in church history. Hundreds of buildings were torn down that had stood for centuries. Men and women were thrown out of monasteries and convents, and the buildings burnt."

"That sounds horrible."

"Oh it was, especially if you considered yourself Catholic. They were convinced the world was ending and that the Protestants were from the devil. But if you were Protestant, you felt the doors were being thrown open and you were finally able to worship in freedom. That's how the United States got settled, in all honesty. Protestants who didn't want any more fighting went there to build a country where everyone could worship as they pleased, even the Catholics."

"Were they all men?"

"No, but those who had the most freedom and education to write were men. Women were involved, but you know... homes and families. Not much time left over to change the world."

"I guess that's why Tricia never got married."

"Mmm, that's one possibility. She certainly couldn't live her vision unless she had someone to share it with her."

"Do you think this Davis guy shared her vision, or at least parts of it? Maybe she wanted him to?"

"I don't think so. She doesn't really talk about him in her journal, so I think the affection was one sided. I think she was one of those women who just didn't want to be married or have children, and since she fought social convention in the church, why not in her personal life? I didn't read anything in her journal showing regrets for focusing on her career instead of having a family."

"For such a modern woman, I just... I dunno. She could have done anything, so why fight with a religion that was never going to treat her like an equal?"

"And just give up? The church wasn't made for men and it shouldn't be controlled by men."

"I guess this hits a little close to home, eh?" Yasmin asked.

"What do you mean?"

"Well, just that you used to do that job and it sounds like you agree with Tricia's fight, and your Aunt wrote all about it and taught Tricia. You could have walked away from the church totally but you didn't. I'm just saying you understand her... what makes her tick."

"Some of it, yes I do. But the different churches are just institutions, like the RCMP or the government or anything else with rules and restrictions, and none of these places would be open to women without fighting for the chance. But the word 'church' itself means everyone is welcome to follow Jesus and believe his teachings, no one is excluded."

"I just don't know why you bother," Yasmin shook her head.

Kendra smiled. She had heard it all before and there weren't enough words in any language to really explain it. It was something each person had to experience on their own. "That's okay. Sometimes I don't either."

"Then..."

Kendra's phone rang to end the conversation. Nodding to the unseen person on the other end, she ended the call and motioned to Jack. "Hugh and Eli have the recording from the debate Wednesday night."

ONCE THEY GATHERED in their borrowed office, Eli turned on the recording. "Now this is the debate that took place Wednesday between our vic, Tricia, and her rapist, Davis."

"Didn't her business partner, ah.. Amanda Morgan, suggest it was a little heated?" Jack asked Kendra.

"Not in so many words, but I definitely understood that to be the case."

"If you consider the guy turning all shades of red as he argued his point, then that would be heated, Kendra," Eli said as he cued the video.

Jesus is male, that's the end of it. You can't argue that point.

No, and I don't intend to. Of course he was male. He had to be male in that society to be heard. No woman had the same freedom to speak in public.

It didn't matter, Jesus was a male because God was a male and therefore all priests must be male.

Jim, that is ridiculous. Even in Genesis, it clearly says 'we will make humans in OUR image'. Plural. You and I were both in Hebrew class the day we learned those words. OUR image, meaning more than one image, meaning male AND female

That only proves that it was plural, a male God and a male Son, there are more than one hence 'our', but it's still male.

Oh please, the plural meant both male and female, and Genesis goes on to say both male and female were created in God's image

Image of love and compassion, not physical image

Then how can you be sure God is male if there isn't a physical image.

"Kendra, here's where you see his temper really flaring."

Kendra nodded at Eli as she continued watching the screen.

God is male! And to further prove that point Jesus came as male. He couldn't have come as a female because he was already male.

Jim, don't you believe in omnipotence?

Of course I do, what kind of question is that?

God came in the form we could deal with at that time, which was a male. Not too rich, but not dirt poor. Educated but not powerful. He came as the son of a middle class carpenter from a distant village and not any of the royal cities. He came as someone who could relate to everyone.

Exactly! HE came so that HE could relate.

The last time he came as male, because he couldn't wander around and talk to people in town otherwise. A young woman wouldn't have been allowed to speak to any man but her husband and other relatives. God had to come as a man to do the job.

Yes, the job only a man could do, which was to represent God to the people.

Even Paul didn't buy that one, Jim. In his letter to Corinth, he said there wasn't male or female. God isn't male or female.

Paul told Corinth the women had to be silent because the men were at worship. That's what Paul had to say on the matter.

Jim, you don't get to rewrite scripture to support your argument. Paul knew a lot of women in ministry who were priests, apostles and missionaries, just like he was. Paul wanted the women to learn and lead because they were equal to men in God's eyes, even if the society of the day didn't believe it.

"Well Kendra, there's our Corinthian's reference. Obviously he thought it was proof," Jack pointed out as Kendra nodded.

Tricia, that's completely beside the point. All of the disciples were male, just as the leaders of the church are to be male.

Then why does the Orthodox and Roman church recognize Mary Magdalene to be the Apostle to the Apostles, giving her authority over the men?

What? That's ridiculous. The Orthodox and Roman churches only have men as priests. You won't find them having a different opinion either. Men are priests alone. That's the way the church wants it. That's the way it is.

No Jim, that's not the way it is at all, and that's not supported by history. Women were always priests, and they still are today. Church after church is recognizing that women are equal to men in everything, including the ordained priesthood. You know, I bet the second coming is going to be a woman, probably handicapped, bisexual and poor, who is going to show people like you how wrong you are.

BLASPHEMY!

"That's the end of the debate, Kendra."

"Go back a little bit, Eli."

"How far?"

"To the start of Tricia's final argument. Put it on slow and watch the audience."

Everyone looked more intently at the screen as heads nodded and hands went into the air.

"Wow, you don't usually see that in this kind of setting," Jack said.

"See what?" Hugh asked.

"The hands rising," Jack pointed at the screen.

"What, like they're about to ask questions?"

"That's not questions, Hugh, that's praising, like they were at a tent revival."

"Yeah, but praising who, God or Tricia?" Theresa asked the hanging question.

"Kendra", Hugh started to chucking without humour, "are you trying to tell me you can see a difference in people's attitudes by the way they put up their hands?"

"Ah, yeah you can," Jack said lazily.

"That's a stretch, and you know it. Look... I took the same body reading courses that the rest of you did, and I can't tell the difference between what they're doing and what any debate would inspire. Sure tempers flared, and our rapists is obviously angry, but that would tell me the audience was full of questions."

"Some perhaps, but that was definitely a sign of worship, Hugh. Look, when was the last time you were at a Pentecostal Assembly?"

"I think she's right," Yasmin added. "I've seen my Grandma and her friends do that. The hand goes up and they're usually laughing or smiling, but they're not asking questions."

"*Et tu*?" Hugh snapped at her.

"Hey... easy," Jack jumped to Yasmin's defense. "Look, we're all getting punch drunk around here. We've been following breadcrumbs and pushing each others buttons, but we're one team. No one's turning on each other.. not now."

Regaining control of the room, Kendra said "Hugh, look at the arms again. Eli, slow it down."

"What am I look for?" Hugh said in a huff.

"Look at the arms going up. When people ask a question, the arm shoots straight up from their shoulder and usually stay that way."

"Yeah... and..."

"And look at these people. The hands are moving in front of them then upwards, elbows still bent, heads nodding, palms facing either forwards or upwards. Some of them are pumping their arms."

"Okay, I see that. So it's not questions, so what?"

"So why is this at a debate? When was the last time you saw a nun doing something like that?"

"You mean aside from Bingo?" Hugh smirked, getting a chuckle from everyone.

"Yeah, besides that. Look, that's Evangelical behaviour."

"I'm going to hate myself for asking this, but what's the difference?"

"Okay," Jack started, "your basic Catholic or Reformer is pretty staid in their worship. They'll kneel, they'll cross themselves, they'll even prostrate themselves on the floor, but they don't show enthusiasm. That's what Evangelicals do. Evangelicals get whooped up, they speak in tongues maybe, they dance sometimes, they sing loudly, and they put their hands up in the air as a sign that God has touched them. That's what these people are doing."

"This is getting enthusiastic?" Hugh pointed at the screen and looked at Jack and Kendra dubiously.

"Oh yeah."

"I've seen more life at a bar, to be perfectly honest with you, Kendra."

Kendra nodded, "Yes... but that's a different sort of gathering. Get a group of people in one room doing this and it's infectious. I've even done it at some Gospel concerts."

"Seriously?" Jack smiled, intrigued to learn something new about his longtime friend.

"Yes... All it would have taken was a few people in that community getting excited by what Tricia said to energize the room. As long as they were open to what she was saying, they would easily be caught up in everything. And it stands to reason that anyone who attended worship where she was presiding, would be open to her argument."

"That's a lot of people, Kendra," Theresa pointed out.

"Do we have any more footage of this debate, Eli? I wish we had something with people's faces."

"Sorry Kendra, this is all we've got and I had to dig to find it on her computer. I don't think Tricia thought this was very important. It didn't even have a description on file, I just found it through the date stamp."

"I wonder... perhaps this was just for old time's sake with Jim? He's quite upset but she's not breaking a sweat. For all intents and purposes she's on home turf, and she's probably expressed these opinions before. So why... why would the crowd get excited like this if it's not new?"

"The debate format might do it. People always like a good fight," Jack suggested.

Kendra nodded thoughtfully.

Crossing his arm and tapping his lower lip, Hugh started. "You think all these people are Christians? Maybe they are '*Triciaians*', here to worship at the feet of their goddess."

"Mmmm.... you've got a point," Kendra said as she tilted her head thoughtfully. "We've been approaching this as people against Tricia as a priest, and we've already found the man who showed himself to be most opposed to her to the point of raping and mutilating her just a day after having this argument. He hated what she was saying, but the crowd loved it. Perhaps we're no longer looking for someone who thought Tricia was ruining the church, but instead we're looking for someone who thought Tricia was redeeming it."

"Crowd, like Palm Sunday?" Jack asked.

"Perhaps, but what did you say the other day Theresa, that whoever did this loved her and hated her? We've already found the person who hated her, even if he did love her a little. But

I think now we're looking for someone who might have, dare I say... worshipped her? Do you think?" she looked up at Jack, then around the room.

"Makes sense," Theresa started. "This is a woman who gave her whole life to the community, right? She spent time with the people there, teaching them and talking to them. She didn't turn anyone away. She always seemed to have little miracles to give them, like shelter, and food, and helping them get clean, and a place for their kids to play like real children. You know, the miracles that really matter to the people everyone seems to forget. If you don't know much about church but you're looking for someone to believe in, that sounds like a Messiah to me."

Jack nodded, "Well said, and I think you've nailed it, Theresa. Tricia was an extension of everything she taught and lived. These people had no idea she had a home in a whole other town, where she could be a different person."

"But she wasn't that different, Jack. She still had toys for the neighbourhood kids and a basement full of storage. She neglected her own yard but made sure things at *Bet-Neshar* were safe and beautiful for everyone."

"If you're right, Kendra. 'Pope Joan' would have had a following. I'll check to see who the permanent residents are. That might give us a clue as to who would have been convinced by her side of the debate."

"Those aren't original ideas," Kendra sighed. "Every one of those points is a chapter in my Aunt's book, and I know for a fact others have been arguing and proving those points for a long time. Tricia felt comfortable in her beliefs because she wasn't alone."

Leaning over to squeeze her shoulders, Jack spoke softly to Kendra. "Knowing Mary didn't get Tricia killed, you know that, right?"

"I know... I do. But I'm not sure I could convince Mary of that point if she was standing here in front of me."

"Mary would be happy that you are finding Tricia's killer. That would matter to her. Look, we found her Judas and her Pilate, now we only got to find her Joseph and her Roman soldier and we'll have the whole story."

"Her who?" Theresa asked.

"Her Roman soldier, that's the person who shoved a sword in her side, and her Joseph of Arimathea, the person who cleaned her body and laid it to rest. In our case, the person who put her on the altar."

"Then who shoved the paper in her mouth?" Theresa questioned. "Who in the story does that?"

"No one, but the paper was in her throat, not her mouth. I'm going to go with Davis, here, for doing the paper because it was his passage, his writing, and his anger. If the body was carried, her mouth could easily fallen open naturally or forced open by someone who wanted it that way, without them seeing the paper. It was dark."

"Makes sense. Anything else that we're missing, aside from the identity of the killer?"

"Just how her body was cleaned." Theresa noted.

Kendra cocked her head, "Yeah, we haven't talked about that yet."

"The RCMP was all over the scene before we got called, and they took the evidence from the back rooms when they found Tricia's body. I'll see what information I can get and what oils or soap they found," Hugh announced, brining their update to a close.

CHAPTER TWELVE

"YESTERDAY ELI SET ME up with the link, so I read through Tricia's journal last night," Jack started as he joined Kendra stared out the window. "Lots of prayers for forgiveness and requests for the people in this community and around her home. A real concern for the kids being dragged down by their parent's situations. A few funerals that really upset her. A wedding or two that probably weren't legal. Occasionally she mentions being with a man, but it's usually all about sex and nothing more."

"Yes, I noticed that when I read parts of her journal. She seemed to be more comfortable as 'Pope Joan' than Tricia Steward," Kendra noted.

"No mention of Davis at all, which is telling. It seems he was definitely more interested in her than vice versa."

"I thought so too. He did travel to her place of business, not the other way around. He was probably someone Tricia could have fun with, but I can't see her ever being interested in someone so against what she wanted to be. She doesn't strike me as needy in the man department."

"No... definitely not. She also talked a lot about doing a lot of the physical work around the *Bet-Neshar*, so she wasn't scared to get her hands dirty."

"You know," Kendra started confidentially, "I wish I had known her. She sounds like the kind of person I would really have enjoyed spending time with."

"Yup, I was thinking the same thing. She really lived what she believed. How many of us can say we have that kind of honesty in our lives?"

"Mmm.... true enough. Anything else?"

"Um, she loved the gifts from your aunt."

"Gifts?"

"Yeah, there was the books, lots of books, not just Mary's but other authors as well."

"I guess I didn't get that far. So nothing in her journal points to anyone who would want her dead or saw her as someone to worship. She didn't even think enough of her rapists to bother talking about him. She didn't see this coming at all."

"Nope. Davis gets a mention when he shows up unannounced, but he's greeted like a long lost brother. Every gift she gets seems to really surprise her. If she's being praised more than usual, it didn't go to her head enough to be written down, so I'm guessing she didn't have a clue. She had her eye on the ball, and didn't notice who had their eye on her."

"Admirable, but not helpful. Alright what about the back room where the oils and soap was found?"

"It was their Sacristy. There were boxes of wine and wafers, candles, table coverings in different colours, some baptismal records, also probably not legit as far as the church is concerned. The investigators lifted prints from the sink and counter, some partials but not enough to get an ID. But the towels and the dirt on the floor matched the rope, so they all came from the same place. And there were traces of blood on the towels that matched Tricia."

"Figures, so... lets walk through this again. Jim shows up for a visit unannounced and Tricia welcomes him like she does everyone else. She gives him a room with a great view, which just happens to be an upper room. Jim sees how the people at *Bet-Neshar* adore her and maybe starts to get jealous, either of Tricia or for himself. He's had condoms in his pocket for how long? He's thinking of how it would be to finally be the one she chooses, but she never chooses him, so somehow he gets his hands on Rohypnol. If she doesn't come willingly, he'll have her another way. The tension builds, then the night comes where they debate each other. No one supports his time-honoured traditional attitudes about women as priests. He's ready to explode and sits on that emotion all day long. Finally the next night, on one of the holiest nights for a Christian, he watches Tricia preside over Eucharist, something she shouldn't be doing but he should and yet no one will give him a church. She probably even washes his feet as a servant. Perhaps he strokes her hair or looks into her eyes, but the love he sees in them is the same look she is giving to everyone else. He either doesn't realize that or he does, and it angers him even more. Just before she presides, they would probably share the Kiss of Peace, and he gets the same kiss everyone else gets. Again, it flares his anger. Once she is finished, he what... leads her to the woods while everyone else is going to bed?"

"He probably gives her the laced drink before hand. There's no sign of resistance out in the woods, and it would be damned cold this time of year."

"Right. He gives her a drink, she feels sleepy so he leads her out for fresh air, into the woods at the back where he's already formed a hideaway just for them. Pillows on the ground and a small fire to give light and warmth. So then... she stumbles, and he places her on the ground. He kisses her and she's completely his for the taking. Does he know she doesn't want children? Is that why he is careful? It would be a way of controlling her and always being linked to him."

"Maybe it's for his own protection. If he's keeping tabs on her he certainly knows she gets around. Maybe he doesn't want to catch anything from her," Jack shrugged the possibility.

"You could be right. He was certainly thinking when he purchased the condoms. Okay, he tears her clothing maybe, at least he exposes her and rapes her. She's probably had enough time with the drugs that she doesn't respond, which would fuel his anger. He wanted her to love him and she's lifeless. He's probably thinking if she wants to live like Jesus, he'll treat her like Jesus. He looks at the fire and sees that spikes were on the edges getting hot, so he grabs one and a stone and bangs it into her hand. That would get a response. Seeing the rope, he ties her to the pillows then grabs another spike to get a similar response. She moans, probably moving a little, and the excitement he feels enables him to rape her a second time. But again no real response to his body. Beyond rage, he ties her legs then takes the last spike and nails it into her ankles. This time though, her reaction is incredible pain, which she hopefully didn't register consciously, and she passes out. He thinks he's killed her and he sobers. What has he done? He starts walking around, tearing his clothing and looking at her. He leans in for one last kiss and feels her cold lips, believing they mean death but really they are cold because of the ground and night air. He doesn't think it through he just wanders off and finds the large tree with more rope underneath, one tied like a noose. At some point he wrote '1 Cor 14:34' on a piece of paper and shoved it into her mouth, and now he writes 'Judas' and puts it around his neck along with the rope. He pulls the tab from his shirt, loses his glasses, stops ripping his own clothing, then climbs the tree to attach the other end of the rope, and falls to his death."

"Yeah, and from that short distance, it wouldn't have been enough to snap his neck, so he choked to death."

Shaking her head, Kendra continued, "Someone either watched or came upon them in the woods. Perhaps they watched the rape and abuse, or maybe they came after the fact. Either way, someone showed up after the damage was done. They untied Tricia's arms and legs and took the spikes out of her body, but when?"

"The rope was left behind, so that was done first. The spikes they took with them. We didn't find them anywhere around the crime scene, so I'm guessing they carried her away with the spikes still in her, which would make the pain enough to keep her unconscious. If Davis thought she was dead, then whoever picked up her body probably thought she was dead too."

"Right," Kendra nodded. "So we're still talking about someone with enough strength to get her out of the woods unseen, and probably around the time Davis' heart was stopping. There were no signs of struggle, and without his glasses he wouldn't have seen anyone else around. Whoever it was, he, she or they took her into the Sacristy, cleaned the dirt from her body and rubbed her with the oil, took the spikes out and kept them, then took her into the chapel and put her on the table."

"Then set the table too, they knew how to do that. The altar would have been cleaned after Maundy Thursday service, so the person or people who put her on the table knew what they were doing."

"Agreed. They laid her down looking upwards, her eyes and mouth open, and shoved a sword into her side, cutting her up inside. Then they positioned the empty chalice by the blood pouring onto the table, or maybe it tipped over when he put Tricia on the table it just fell that way. Either way anyone coming in would see the table had been set. They lit the candle, and then left, taking the stakes and whatever Tricia had been wearing with them."

"Yup," Jack said as he looked out the window.

A knock on the office door surprised both of them.

"Kendra..." Theresa stood looking from Jack and Kendra to the new arrivals.

"Yes? Can I help you?" Kendra asked, moving forward to welcome their guests.

The two older women looked excited and hopeful. Their clothing was nondescript and looked like it had been picked from the cast-off bag sometime in the last century. Looking down at their shoes, Kendra saw matching grey shoes, sensible and strikingly similar to the ones worn by nuns and nurses. With them was a young man who seemed agitated and didn't share the excitement of his companions.

"Yes, we're here to see Pope Joan," one of the women announced as she moved forward.

"Pope Joan?" Kendra was surprised, and quickly looked at the others in the room.

"Joan, dear," the second woman started calling as she walked further in the room, "we're here. You can come out now."

"I'm sorry...." Kendra started, "there's been a bit of a misunderstanding. Joan isn't here with us."

"Oh... then just tell us where she is, and we'll take her home."

"Excuse me," Jack started towards the two woman, "but Joan is dead."

"Oh yes, we know that," the second woman nodded. "We were there, weren't we," she looked to the others and nodded. "But she's alive now and we've come to take her home."

"It's the third day," the young man explained, then he held up his bundle to show spikes hidden in the material."

Kendra and Jack looked at each other, then back to the bundle in the young man's arms. "May I see that?" Kendra asked, holding her arms out.

"No," he said, and folded it back towards his body, and looked around the room anxiously.

"Okay," Kendra said, pulling her hands back. Then she turned to the woman who had been searching. "And you are?"

"I'm Sister Leah," she answered, still full of anticipation, "and this is Sister Shirley, and Timmy, our house boy."

"*Timmy* our house boy", Hugh mouthed to the others in the room, then wrote down the name.

"Sister Leah, I'm Kendra Ward and this is Jack Hudson. Would you mind sitting down so we can talk?"

"Of course, that would be fine. But this won't take too long, will it?"

"Not at all."

While Kendra sat down with the two older woman, Jack stood behind them. He looked casual but she knew Jack's hand was close to his gun and he would pull it out if he needed to protect her. The young man stayed close to the door, his eyes darting back and forth as though he was wary of being startled.

"It's very nice to finally meet you," Sister Leah started immediately. "I saw you. I saw you enter the chapel after Joan was found. You looked right at home. I can always tell. I knew you would take good care of her. When can I see her? When can we see Joan?"

"We have to get a few things cleared up first. What can you tell us about the night Joan died?" Kendra started.

"Oh, many things. What would you like to know?"

"Why didn't you talk to us when we got here?" Jack asked.

"We couldn't, we made a vow. But today is Easter Sunday and it's time to celebrate!"

Jack rolled his eyes slightly and looked at Kendra, who matched him with a raised eyebrow.

"How about you tell us what happened from the beginning. Starting with Maundy Thursday service," Kendra began, turning back to the the table

"Oh yes, I can tell you about that. Pope Joan was beautiful as ever. You know, she admitted who she was the night before. I always suspected, but when she let it slip that Christ would come again as a woman, I knew. I knew down to my toes. We had been waiting for so long, and here she was. I always knew God would come again as a woman and I prayed it would be in my lifetime. Oh how I prayed. And the way Joan explained it. I knew the devil was right beside her saying everything was wrong. The devil tempts people, you know. But Jesus didn't give into temptation, and neither did Joan. She smiled and we knew. We knew! And we were right. That devil led her out after the service.

"We were watching, "Sister Shirley picked up the story, as Sister Leah stood beside her agreeing happily. We saw him. He worked his wiles on her and she leaned into him. He lead her away just like the devil led Jesus two thousands years ago. He led her into Gethsemane and he kissed her, just like Judas did before. And he accused her and he tortured her, just like before. She didn't protest, not one bit. She took the torture. It wasn't a crown of thorns and beating this time. Nope. Pope Joan always told us torture to a woman was different that torture to a man, and she was tortured. He took from her what every man tries to take from a woman, and she let him. She didn't fight. And he got mad... he got real mad."

Sister Leah interrupted, "That devil in his black, he was ready. He put her on the cross, and he banged those spikes into her. He said all sorts of ungodly things to her. Tied her up right good, then he tortured her again. But still she held strong and didn't give him what he wanted.

"I went back to get Timmy, and we went back to the garden to get our Lord. She was lying still. The devil was gone but he had finished the job by tying her feet and nailing them to the cross too."

"A cross?" Jack asked. "What did it look like?"

"Oh, it weren't wood like last time. No, this time it was soft white pillows. Can you imagine? Pillows? I guess when you torture a woman like that devil did, it's supposed to be done somewhere soft. Anyway, it was shaped like a cross so that's what mattered.

"Joan was just lying there, beautiful as ever. There was some blood you know, where the devil hurt her, but the rest was pure white like the moon. Sister Shirley pulled Timmy along. He does errands for us. Anyway, we untied Joan's body just like they did Jesus' body, and we took her to get cleaned up. Last time you know, there were no women around so the body wasn't done up proper for Easter morning. This time we made sure we did everything just right. We took her clothes off, they were ripped anyway, and cleaned up that blood mess. Timmy pulled those spikes out. He's a strong boy and he did it like it was nothing. Then we covered her with oil, the way Mary Magdalene wanted to do the last time but she didn't have the chance. And we put her on the table, just as she said. Christ was the sacrifice. We told Timmy to open her eyes so she was looking up to heaven, waiting to see God face to face."

Kendra and Jack looked at each other, then looked back at Sister Leah, who had crossed her hands over her heart, looking almost angelic.

"And then what happened?" Kendra prompted her.

"Then what?" Sister Leah looked confused. "Then we said a prayer and returned to our sisters to keep vigil until sunrise on the third day. We didn't know how it would happen, this being a different time and all, but we knew the third day she would rise again. So when are we going to get her?"

Trying again, Jack prompted her, "We found the table set for Eucharist."

"Oh that... that was Sister Shirley's idea. She thought if we were laying out the sacrifice, we should prepare the table to receive it too." Sister Leah touched Sister Shirley's arm, they both looked pleased with themselves.

"She was beside the chalice and paten, not on them," Kendra clarified.

"Well yes, we couldn't very well have her sitting on the stuff when we still had to collect the blood now, could we?" Sister Leah looked at them as though they had asked the most ignorant question possible.

"And what blood did you collect?"

"I thought you understood the way God worked?" Sister Leah looked at Kendra and balked. "I think I'm done answering your questions. I'm wanting to see my Lord now."

"Wouldn't that be 'Lady'?" Jack couldn't help ask.

"Christ is Lord of all," she answered, then sat back in her chair, arms crossed. The interview was over.

"Would you mind waiting here, and thank you for telling us what you witnessed." Kendra said as she and Jack got up and left the room.

Outside the door Kendra put her hand on her forehead and closed her eyes.

"I wasn't expecting that," Jack started.

"Nor was I, but we still don't have the killer. She didn't say anything about how Tricia was sliced through the side."

"These nuns are a piece of work. How can anyone watch a rape and assumed murder and think it was predestined?" Jack asked.

Kendra shook her head, "Others have been just as deluded. What about the boy, Timmy?"

"You think he's the one who will tell us about the cut to her side?" Jack asked.

Opening the door again they entered the room to find the two looking expectant.

Timmy showed he was scared for the first time. "She's alive already, I know that. She moved. I saw her. She was dead then she come back and I made sure she was dead and now she will come back again. She's haunting me, isn't she."

"Too easy," Jack whispered to Kendra.

CHAPTER THIRTEEN

TIMMY STARTED PACING back and forth while Kendra asked Theresa to take their guests out to the lobby of the station. Once Sister Leah and Sister Shirley had left the room, she sat down and asked Timmy to sit down as well. Jack resumed his place as casual guard.

"I like moving," Timmy said, "it helps me think."

"Okay, if it is easier for you. Can you tell us what happened the other night, Timmy. What happened after you and the sisters found Pope Joan?"

"She looked kinda scary with the moon shinning on her. There was a fire close by, but I knocked that out with my foot. She was all blue and purple and white. She looked like a ghost. And she was cold, that's how come we knew she was dead. The sisters untied everything and told me to carry her. I never touched nothing dead before, not even my dog when he got run over. I picked her up, but I felt someone watching me. I turned around scared and seed him. I seed the devil.

"Anyways, I went with them into the back door, carrying her body. The sisters washed her up, got rid of the blood that was on her secret place, and they asked me to take out the nails. Good thing they were big, 'cause they came right out like nothing. I put them on the dress so they wouldn't get scratched. They were good nails and I could use them again. I found a whole pile of them out by the old fence they tore down last Fall. Guess I didn't see these ones when I picked them up.

"Anyways, once they cleaned her, they found some oil and put it all over her. It smelled bad, but they said it was the good stuff. I don't know about stuff like that. And they kept saying God wanted this to happen and God was keeping promises, and stuff like that. I'm not even sure God is real, but they sure think so.

"Anyways, I carried her into the chapel like they told me and put her on the big table. Then the sisters went back into room on the side to get matches for the candle. I opened her eyes like Sister said, and she moved. She was dead and she moved. I got so scared, I just grabbed my sword and shoved it in her to stop. I wasn't having no back-from-the-dead haunt me like that."

"You have a sword?" Kendra asked. "Do you keep it with you all the time?"

"Nah, it's not safe to have that in daylight. Someone might steal it. I only take it with me when I'm running errands after dark."

"Timmy, why were you at *Bet-Neshar* so late? Did you live there?"

"Nah, but sometimes I stay over if I'm going to be out past my curfew. Sister Shirley lets me have one of the rooms."

"What were you doing with the sister so late, Timmy?" Kendra asked kindly.

"I don't feel like talking about it."

"About what, Timmy?"

"I'll get the sister in trouble. I don't want to talk about it."

"It's alright, Timmy."

"No it's not. She's already in trouble because of it. I don't want to tell you," Timmy was getting more worked up, even though Kendra was trying to calm him. Jack was ready to move but Kendra signaled for him to keep his place.

"You were delivering something you shouldn't have touched, weren't you Timmy. Something Sister Shirley asked you to get."

"The devil made her do it," Timmy screamed at her and pounded the table.

"What did the devil look like?"

"He's watching me. I saw him in the tree. He's watching me. He's going to come back and kill me too, I know it. I know it."

Kendra looked at Jack as she stood. "Did the devil ask for white pills, Timmy?"

"YOU'RE EVIL!" he screamed, shoving at the table then lunged towards Kendra. Timmy grabbed Kendra around the neck and started to squeeze.

Jack had been ready and rushed towards Timmy, pulling him from Kendra and pushed him over the edge of the table. It took both Jack and Hugh, who had been slowly walking towards the table, to grab Timmy's arms behind his back to place the cuffs. Kendra watched gasping.

"YOU CAN GO TO HELL!" Timmy continued yelling. "I'M NOT TELLING YOU NOTHING."

"Who had the pills Timmy?" Kendra pushed again. "How did the devil get the pills?"

"NO!" Timmy screamed again, but already the fight was leaving him. "No..." he said, starting to cry.

"Where Timmy?"

Sobbing, he shook his head, "No... no, it makes him happy."

"Makes who happy?" Hugh asked gently. "Who has the white pills to make him happy."

"He did... the devil did. He brought 'em. He had everything in his Bible. Sister Shirley, she told me to go get it."

"Did Sister Shirley tell you what it was?" Huge pushed further.

Shaking his head violently from side to side, tears running down his cheeks, Timmy pulled at his cuffs.

"She just said I was the messenger and I had to make sure it happened just right when they went out to pray. The devil did his part, the sisters did their part and I carried Pope Joan from station to station, even when she couldn't move herself. My job was to get everyone what they needed, and the devil needed his white pills. He forgot to get them before the service so Sister Shirley told me to get them. It was late so I took my sword. The houses are scary at night." Timmy started sobbing again, "She got alive too soon.... too soon, that's all."

"Timmy, no!" Sister Shirley called across the lobby and rushed to his side. Jack had been leading the handcuffed young man across the lobby to the other side of the building to be processed.

Once Timmy was secured, Jack walked over to them and glared. "He just finished what you started, didn't he Sister Shirley." She backed up in surprise, right into the Hugh who was waiting with at second pair of handcuffs.

"What? Why are you doing this?" Sister Shirley cried, trying to push free. "I didn't do anything wrong."

Hugh snorted, "Yeah, aiding and abetting, failure to report a crime, possibly dealing in illegal substances, and probably some murder charges, but we'll let the RCMP and crown attorney decide on that one."

"What?" Sister Shirley asked again, colour draining from her face. "No... no, you have it all wrong."

"Yeah.... somehow we always do," Hugh grunted as he pushed the older woman towards the door where they had led Timmy moments before.

KENDRA PLACED THE PICTURES from the morgue in front of Sister Leah, Sister Margaret and Amanda.

"I thought you said she didn't suffer," Amanda accused, tracing Tricia's face with her fingertip.

"Her body suffered, but she wouldn't have been aware of it," Yasmin said gently.

"And she would be alive if Timmy...." Sister Leah couldn't finish.

"Yes, with horrible scars in her hands and ankles, and she would have needed surgery to repair the damage, but she would have lived."

"But... she was our Saviour. She was the second coming."

Amanda had had enough, and turned on the sister. "Her name was Tricia, and she wasn't your saviour or the second anything. She was an idealist who made some bad choices, and was betrayed by people she trusted. There might even be more charges laid against you!"

Getting up, Amanda stormed out of the room. The two sisters were not far behind her, but moved more slowly. Both looking much older and hunched over than they had been before.

"TIMMY AND SISTER SHIRLEY could always plead insanity," Eli offered, coming to lean against the window beside Kendra.

"I don't see that happening," Jack shook his head. "Those two knowingly and willingly stood by while a woman was raped, tortured and one of them murdered her. I can't see the Crown ignoring any of that. Religious fanaticism is not an insanity defense."

"What do you think will happen, Kenny?" Hugh asked as he sagged down in the seat beside the front door.

"They will both be sent for a psychiatric assessment, and I seriously doubt either will be found Not Criminally Responsible. This was a crime that could have been stopped so many times before it actually happened, and it wasn't."

"What do they say about hindsight?" Theresa offered, bringing a nod of acknowledgement from the group.

After a few moments of silence Kendra looked around. "Okay everyone, it's Easter and we all have other places we want to be. Jack and I will finish the paperwork so you go home and do your thing. And don't take it personally but I hope we don't have to see each other for a long time... at least not like this."

Nods of agreement and hugs passed between the six, and they headed off towards the hotel to collect their belongings and headed home to salvage some of the holiday. Jack put his arm around Kendra's shoulder and pulled her to his side as they watched the others leave the station.

Once everyone was gone he picked a book from the table and handed it to her. "I know this isn't a memory you want along side of the good times with your Aunt Mary, but here... take this."

Kendra looked down at the book and turned it over. Inside the front cover he had placed a picture of Tricia and Mary together.

Smiling at the picture, Kendra traced the faces. "Could I have been her?"

"What?" Jack asked.

"Tricia," Kendra replied looking up at him seeking reassurance. "In another time and place could I have been Tricia.'

"Nope," Jack shook his head with conviction. "Not a chance. You help people but you've always been smart about it. You never meet people alone, you always suggest the help from doctors or lawyers rather than figuring it out yourself, and you aren't naive about people. Tricia was and she paid for it."

"She's not to blame for what happened."

"No she isn't, but if I had been around when she was alive, I would have had a long list of things for her to do so she could live her dream and live it safely. You've got my list and you make sure you're covered."

Kendra looked down at the picture again and sighed.

Jack tapped the picture to get her attention, "You know the two women in that picture would be mighty proud of you right. You know what happened here, so do something with it. Let her make things better for other women. You've got a gift Kenny. Make sure you tell Tricia's story."

About the Author

Deborah Suddard has been telling stories her whole life, to the young and old alike. She combines her talent as a storyteller with her study of history and Biblical studies, to give readers a fuller picture of what women's faith life really looked like in the past. When she is not writing, Deborah spends her time as a speaker, homeschooling mother, and furthering her academic career. Broken For You is her first pubished book.

www.ingramcontent.com/pod-product-compliance
Ingram Content Group UK Ltd.
Pitfield, Milton Keynes, MK11 3LW, UK
UKHW020225250726
13967UKWH00001B/189

9 781386 865070